ADVAN(
POCKETS OF PROMISE

"With her debut novel, *Pockets of Promise*, Laurie Stroup Smith has elevated a lovely Amish romance to a universal coming-of-age story. Against the beautiful backdrop of sunny Pinecraft, FL, Smith explores the complicated emotions experienced by Mariah Mast as she tries to make some of the most important decisions of her life. Only eighteen, Mariah's *Rumspringa* is filled with the same deep potholes as her English counterparts—parties, alcohol, romance, and future endeavors. Only this Plain woman must also decide whether to join her church or break away and find herself far from home and family. Sweet notes from her grandma help Mariah find her way. The result is a satisfying story of how God places people in our lives, sometimes only for a season, but always for a reason."

—Kelly Irvin, award-winning author of *Mountains of Grace and a Long Bridge Home*

"A fresh new voice in Amish fiction...Smith pulls us straight into the confusion of an Amish rumspringa...touching, authentic, and sweet."

—Vannetta Chapman, award-winning author of *Agatha's Amish B&B Series*

"Charming, sweet, and entertaining, Laurie Stroup Smith's debut will leave warmth in your heart and a smile on your face! Mariah's journey to finding - and living out - her purpose is honest and relatable, and readers will enjoy peeking over her shoulder as she discovers the special words of wisdom from her grandmother. The smooth, easy flow of the author's writing style adds to everything I loved about this story. Laurie Stroup Smith is a delightful new voice in Amish fiction, and fans of the genre will want to add this to their must-buy list!"

—Carrie Schmidt, *Reading is My Superpower*

POCKETS OF PROMISE

BOOK 1 IN THE AMISH KEEPSAKE QUILT SERIES

LAURIE STROUP SMITH

For Dad
I will always remember:
"Ask and it will be given to you; seek and you will find;
knock and the door will be opened to you."
Matthew 7:7

CHAPTER ONE

Mariah couldn't get past the smell. And yet, she lifted the red plastic cup to her lips and pretended to drink the foamy liquid. The bass drum bumped in her chest as smoke from the bonfire swirled to the heavens and tickled her nose. Sniffling, she shifted her hips against the truck's rear bumper. The new acquaintance sitting beside her removed his leather jacket, pushed up his sleeves, and put a strong arm around her.

"Happy Birthday." He leaned close and kissed her cheek. "Eighteen, right?" The beer on his breath collided with his strong cologne.

She nodded as her stomach churned. With an audible sigh, she ran her hand over the soft denim covering her thighs. Lydia had been right—the stiff pair of jeans did loosen. An hour earlier, her best friend had danced into the crowd and disappeared. Ready to go home, Mariah squinted to focus on the field's dark corners, which hid in the shadows, untouched by the moon and stars.

"Look at you, neighbor." Lydia twirled toward the parked pickup. Her faded jeans accented her curves, and makeup disguised her natural beauty. Tripping on a stick in the hay, she spilled a can of beer on her arm, and then licked her wrist and laughed. "Havin' fun, birthday girl?"

Mariah raised the cup toward her best friend but remained silent.

"So, I guess you've met Dustin?" Lydia nudged her with an elbow.

"Oh, we've met all right." He fingered her hair all the way down her back and rested his hand on her hip.

She shuddered.

"Like that, do ya?" He nibbled her ear, and his scruffy chin scratched her cheek.

Squirming out of his grasp, she rose from her seat on the tailgate and readjusted the tight jeans. "Don't you think it's about time to get back home?"

Her friend clicked a button on her cell phone—the phone she hid from her parents. "It's not even midnight. It's your birthday. It took me two years, but I finally convinced you to come out to enjoy your *Rumspringa*. Live a little, would ya?" She moved her hips to the beat of a new song.

The reflection of flames flickered in Dustin's dark eyes, his focus locked on Mariah. "Hey, I thought you wanted to go on a ride with me." He lifted his chin toward the Harley he claimed to have borrowed from his dad.

"Maybe another time. But *danke*—I mean, thank you for the offer."

"Take me!" Lydia jumped and raised her arms. The firelight tickled her exposed belly.

Dustin's eyes widened. "Let's go, girlie." Standing, he grabbed her hand.

Mariah touched her friend's arm. "Wait. How will I get home?"

"Josiah's still here. I saw him talking with friends a few

minutes ago. I'm sure he'd *love* to give you a ride home." She spun into Dustin's open arms. "Don't worry about me. I'll have this big guy drop me off at home—or not." She winked.

Dustin buried his face in Lydia's neck, which caused her to squeal.

"But we should stay together." Her voice wavered.

"It's fine."

Stepping closer, Mariah whispered, "You don't even really know him, do you?"

"I said, it's fine." Lydia glared at her and thinned her lips. "Josiah's over there." She jerked her head toward a group of teens to her left.

"Be careful."

Her best friend followed Dustin's muscular form from the fire's warm glow into the chill of the darkness.

Scanning the crowd, Mariah wrung her fingers and took hesitant steps in search of Josiah. Girls she knew had painted their faces with makeup. Their hair, which had never touched a pair of scissors, spilled over their shoulders, making it difficult to recognize familiar faces. In the bonfire's golden light, she spotted three girls in cranberry-colored dresses near a row of buggies and hustled for fear she would miss a ride home.

"Having fun?" she asked, peering at her friends from behind the buggy.

"Mariah?" Josiah's sister embraced her. "Look at you. Your hair." She bounced the curly locks in her palm. "Too bad you have to keep those beautiful brown curls hidden under a *kapp*. What a shame." Her big brown eyes fought to focus as a hiccup escaped through her parted lips.

"Happy Birthday." Stepping back, she lost her balance and swiped the long blond strands of hair out of her face.

Josiah extended an arm to help her remain upright.

"There's one in every bunch, ain't so?" He rolled his eyes.

Mariah giggled. In contrast to Dustin's flashy grin, Josiah's familiar smile warmed her. Even in firelight's glow, his bright blue shirt accented his beautiful eyes. Growing up, she'd come home from school and talk about the two boys in her class named Josiah. Her mother kept the stories straight, but only if she referred to Josiah Weaver as Josiah Blue Eyes.

"So, are you heading home any time soon?" she asked.

"Hadn't planned on it." He leaned against the buggy. "Why? Need a ride?"

"If you have room?"

"What happened to your new *friend*?" Those baby blues darkened.

She wrung her fingers again, this time until her knuckles cracked. "He and Lydia went for a ride."

"You didn't wanna go with them?"

"No, I'm ready to go home."

Tipping back a red cup, he took a long gulp.

"Are you drinking beer?"

"Really?" He dropped his chin and tilted the cup toward her. "Sprite and apple juice."

"I should've known."

He pulled on his sister's sleeve. "I'm headin' out now. Gonna take Mariah home. If you're coming, could you sit in the back?"

As his sister stumbled into the buggy, Josiah offered Mariah his hand. "You can sit up front with me."

Once she had settled in her seat, Josiah untied his ebony gelding from the hitching post. The animal pawed the ground with his front right hoof and neighed, a fog of breath escaped his nostrils.

Turning toward his sister seated behind her, she asked,

"Where's your boyfriend?"

"His uncle passed away." Her words slurred. "And he's helping out at their farm in Sugarcreek for a few months."

"I'm sorry. I bet it's hard to be apart. Do you enjoy coming to these parties together?"

"Sometimes, but my crowd prefers to play volleyball or go bowling." She yawned, her eyelids losing their fight to stay open. "I'm tired. Think I'm gonna rest for a minute."

Mariah faced forward as Josiah climbed in beside her and gave his horse a signal to move.

"Stubborn horse." He shook the reins. "Tch-tch. Let's go, Pete." With heavy steps, the Standardbred pulled the buggy forward. "How about you? Did you enjoy your first field party?"

She shrugged.

"Happy Birthday, by the way." Clearing his throat, he nodded toward the fire, where the pickup truck remained parked. "Looked like you were having a mighty *gut* time with the *Englisher*."

Heat rushed to her cheeks, and the tips of her ears burned.

"To be honest, I—I didn't. And I don't know what you think you saw, but—" She paused, and his sister's snore filled the silence. "I didn't enjoy my time here tonight. *Danke* for taking me home." She fingered the lace trim on the top she had borrowed from the clothes hidden in the back of Lydia's closet.

"Like you, I didn't have much fun either." They slowed to a stop at an intersection. "I struggled the entire time from wanting to punch that guy for touching you."

"Josiah. You tend to let your anger get the best of you, but you know that's not our way. I'm glad you had some sense."

"Well then, you'll be glad to hear I prayed instead this time that he wouldn't hurt you."

A car's headlights shone into the buggy, illuminating their faces. The twin beams twinkled in his eyes. He reached for her hand and gave it a soft squeeze, then re-gripped the reins.

Since they were young, Josiah had served as her protector. She recalled the day he walked her home from school, and they found shattered glass near the barn. The police got involved to investigate the robbery, and she was more scared than she'd ever been. Josiah stayed by her side through the entire ordeal. Once again, he had rescued her from an uncomfortable situation. She lowered her head.

A cool gust of wind whipped her hair around her neck. She gasped and grabbed her bare head. "My *kapp*." She grasped her legs covered in tight denim. "My dress. I left them in the other buggy."

"What other buggy?"

"I rode to the party with Lydia and one of her other friends. Before she took off, she told me to catch a ride home with you. I forgot all about my clothes. I can't go home in these jeans." She clapped her hands over her mouth.

"Whose jeans are those—Lydia's?" When Mariah nodded, he continued, "It's your *Rumspringa*. Your parents will understand a night out in jeans."

"I'm not so sure."

"Plus, they'll be asleep when you get home."

"How could I have been so irresponsible?" Tears welled up her eyes. The few sips of beer she had managed to swallow caused her emotions to rise. "First the *Englisher*, then you, then my dress and *kapp*." She crumpled toward her lap.

Josiah steered the buggy off the main highway onto a dirt road. Moonlight draped the blunt stumps of cornstalks in a dim sheet of light. "Don't worry. I'll fix this for you."

"What do you mean?"

"We can stop at my house before I take you home. I'll get my sister inside, and I can grab one of her dresses for you to borrow. Return it to her at church on Sunday."

She wiped her nose with the back of her hand. "You would go to all that trouble for me?"

He gave the reins a gentle tug and stopped the buggy in front of his family's home, the house needing a fresh coat of white paint. "For you, nothing could be trouble. Now, for that one," he tilted his head toward the back seat where his sister stretched and moaned. "Nothing but trouble." He leaned over the seat and shook her. "Wake up. We're home."

As he supported his sister up the steps to their porch and helped her unlock the front door, Mariah noted how his shirt stretched over his strong shoulders. His sister stumbled into the house by her own efforts, and he followed.

For you, nothing could be trouble. His words echoed in her thoughts. He had always been attentive to her needs, but she'd never thought of him as anything other than a dear friend. Until now. Could Josiah Weaver be the husband she'd prayed for? Could their friendship develop into the romantic relationship she'd pictured in her dreams?

Gravel crackled beneath heavy footsteps—intentional steps that, at this moment, were directed toward her. He straightened his hat and returned to the seat beside her. The hair on her arms stood up, and she trembled.

"You cold?" Reaching over, he grabbed a wool blanket from the floor, which he then draped across her shoulders. "Now let's get you some real clothes," he said with a wink.

"I don't know how I can thank you for taking such *gut* care of me. I don't feel like I deserve all this." She smoothed the blanket on her lap.

"You don't have to thank me. But how 'bout you promise not to go to any more of those parties—unless escorted by me?"

"I don't know if I ever want to go to another party like that. I wasn't comfortable there—too much, too fast."

"You don't understand what I'm saying. Let me be clear. I would love nothing more than to court you. Do I have permission to call on you?"

"Josiah, I don't—" Her mouth went dry.

CHAPTER TWO

Two days after the party, Mariah rose later than expected—even by her standards. She'd faked a stomach bug so she didn't have to face Josiah at church—a trick she'd learned from a character in one of Lydia's romance novels, but she couldn't miss a day of work for confusion of the heart.

Josiah hadn't been able to hide his disappointment when she didn't answer his invitation to court with a resounding yes. How could she? She'd never considered him to be more than a friend, not that she couldn't imagine her feelings for him could grow. Prayers for clarity occupied a great deal of her Sunday, and her week started with similar thoughts.

She hurried to get dressed and rushed out the front door. A gentle breeze rustled the trees, and she walked out of her way to step on a leaf, satisfied with the crunch beneath her shoe. She filled her lungs with fresh fall air and smiled, arriving at the end of the gravel driveway with one minute to spare. The driver wouldn't have to honk the horn today.

As if he could hear her thoughts, Carl rounded the corner and stopped the van in front of her. She smoothed her dress and then opened the passenger door.

The older man in the driver's seat wore his usual uniform—black pants, a white collared shirt, and his red nylon varsity jacket, which Mariah estimated to be at least forty years old. "*Gut matin*, Carl."

"Good morning, Sunshine. I thought for sure I'd be waiting on you—with your big birthday this weekend and all. Setting a trend now that you're eighteen?"

"Don't get your hopes up. This may not happen again any time soon." She giggled and buckled her seat belt.

He shifted the van into drive. "Well, it's probably good your parents agreed to let you work for Mr. Byler then. Not sure you could make the early commute to the bakery with the rest of your family."

"That's true." She balled her fists. "They weren't thrilled with the idea at first, but I did not want to bake fried pies and cinnamon rolls for the rest of my life anyway."

The man's cell phone rang, and Mariah pushed aside the memories stirred up by the mention of her decision to work at the hardware store—a good match for her. Instead, she relaxed into her seat for the three-mile ride into town. As her driver steered past rolling hills dotted with farms and grazing cattle, she created a mental checklist for the day, but then her thoughts returned to the conversation she'd had with Josiah after the party.

Words held incredible power when spoken, but what remained unsaid could have also caused pain. She didn't want to hurt him, but to misrepresent her true feelings didn't seem right either. She had chosen honesty. What if God intended her to marry someone she had not yet met? The man of her dreams might not even be Amish. What would that mean for her? For her relationship with her family and friends?

The driver pulled the van to a stop next to the curb on the corner outside the hardware store. Across the street, a long line of customers waited for their turn to enter her family's bakery. She stepped onto the sidewalk and offered her thanks with a wave and then turned right to enter the back door of the one-story red brick building.

Relieved to enter the quiet store, she popped her head into Mr. Byler's tidy office to alert him of her arrival. As usual, she found him huddled over his desk, wearing light-blue shirt and dark trousers held up by navy suspenders. His black-brimmed hat sat on a filing cabinet next to the desk.

"*Gut* morning, Mr. Byler. Cut yourself shaving again?" She stifled a laugh.

"Oops." He peeled the small wad of tissue from the nick beneath his nose and tossed it in the trash. "What would I do without you keeping me in line?" Looking at her through his silver-rimmed glasses, the store owner stroked his graying beard.

She smiled. "I'll unlock the door and flip our Open sign."

"This store might not stay in business if not for you." He swiveled his chair and faced a pile of papers on his desk.

With the overhead lights switched on, she hurried between the aisles, weaving her way to the front of the store. Reaching the front counter, she grabbed her orange apron from a hook near the register and tied the strings behind her back. Out of habit, she tucked a pen next to the calculator in the left pocket of her apron and patted the right pocket for a notepad. The bells on the door jingled, and a gust of crisp air rushed into the store. She shivered and pulled a gray cardigan over her dress.

"Welcome to Byler's." Mariah smiled at an older woman carrying an oversized purse trimmed with shiny gold beads.

"Good morning, dear. I'm looking for clay pots."

"Aisle eight. I could show you, if you'd like."

The woman waved as she passed the register, so Mariah turned her attention to a stack of order receipts her boss had placed on the counter for her to sort by date. As she shuffled receipts into organized piles, a pair of boots clicked in no particular hurry across the floor.

Searching for an order date on the slip of paper in her hand, she kept her eyes focused on the receipt. The footsteps stopped near the register. "How may I help you?" she asked.

"How you feelin'?"

She held her breath. A shiver rippled through her body as she raised her eyes, greeted by the shiny white smile of none other than Dustin Verona.

"Um, why would I feel anything but great on this beautiful fall morning?" She scanned the store for Mr. Byler. Would her boss remain in his office until she could get rid of this guy? Could he hear their conversation from his desk?

Dustin adjusted a pair of mirrored sunglasses on his head. "Did you have fun the other night?"

She lowered her voice. "It was okay."

"Just okay? I wish you'd gone for a ride with me. When I got back, you weren't there." He placed both hands on the counter and bent close to her—close enough she could smell his cinnamon chewing gum. Close enough to embarrass her should her boss catch sight of them standing together.

Dustin Verona was one of God's most beautiful creations—tall, dark, and handsome like she pictured the heroes in the stories she borrowed from Lydia's bookshelf. Nervous energy clouded her curiosity. Beads of sweat collected along her hairline.

"You should come out to the Bontrager farm on Friday. I

work with those boys, and we're gonna set up back in their fields at dusk. That's why I'm here. I'd like to get a few charcoal grills for the party."

"Follow me." The distance between their bodies grew, allowing her to focus on the task at hand. As they walked past shelves stocked with bird houses and hoses, his boots clunked on the linoleum floor, drowning out the sound of her soft-soled sneakers. "What're you looking for?" She pointed at the inventory to her right. "We have portable kettle grills and portable tabletop grills." Turning to her left, she showed him alternatives. "These models are larger, have burners, and additional features, but they'd be harder to transport, of course."

She reached for the calculator in her pocket and punched random buttons to pass the time. This way she wouldn't get caught staring at him as he made a decision.

He stepped closer to the portable kettle grills and tipped a box on its side, then clicked his tongue and rubbed his chin. "I'll take three of these bad boys. And I'll need a large bag of charcoal. Let me grab a longbed cart. I can get this."

"*Danke*, I mean thank you." She shoved her hands in the apron pockets. "I'll meet you up front."

Moments after she assumed her position at the register, the older woman unloaded her cart on the counter. Mariah entered the price of a dozen clay pots on the keypad, wrapped them in newspaper, and slid them into a plastic shopping bag.

Dustin wheeled his cart to a stop behind the woman and then thumbed through a car and truck magazine. Though Mariah knew a handful of Amish guys who saved money for a used vehicle to drive around during their *Rumspringa*, Mr. Byler made sure to have the magazines in stock for his English customers. Josiah had never expressed any interest in replacing his buggy, and this realization made her glad he wasn't like the other guys she knew.

She tallied the older woman's bill and then turned her attention back to the customer. "Looks like you'll be staying busy for a while."

"I plan to make the pots into Santa, Rudolph, and his elves." Her eyes widened. "Saw the idea on Pin—on the internet." She patted her purse. "Oh, I do apologize. I imagine you don't have the foggiest idea about computers."

Mariah pressed her lips together and hid her hot cheeks. If Dustin heard the woman, he didn't react. What would this customer say if she knew Mr. Byler asked her to track his inventory on various spreadsheets? What would the woman do if she explained that her boss had her place online orders on a regular basis? She forced a smile. "Have a wonderful day. Please visit us again."

Standing on her tiptoes, she craned her neck in time to see Mr. Byler come out of his office. He carried a clipboard and disappeared into the stockroom. This morning he'd stay busy counting the surplus of various fasteners they carried. She relaxed her shoulders and faced Dustin. "Go ahead and leave everything in the cart. I'll ring up the price here."

He leaned against the counter. "Think you'll join us in the field Friday night?"

She shrugged, then consulted the store ad and punched the sale price for the grills. "Your total is $109.14."

"It's gonna be *legendary*." He handed her a wad of $20 bills.

"I don't know. My friends and I have plans to go bowling. You could join us, if you want?"

"Bowling? Sheesh." He curled his lip. "You don't wanna

miss the last big blast this fall

for bowling."

"Well—" The words got stuck between her thoughts and her tongue.

Mr. Byler approached the counter with a bag of washers and bolts in each hand.

She thrust the money into Dustin's hand. "Here's your change."

"See you then?" He winked and then raised his voice. "Good morning. How are you today, sir?"

"Busy as usual with all the harvest festivals and fall projects." Mr. Byler extended his hand toward the display of fertilizer and autumnal lawn decorations and then stroked his thin beard.

"I bet. Well, I best get to work myself." Dustin pushed the cart toward the exit but turned and made direct eye contact with her. "See ya."

"Have a nice day," she said, glancing at her boss, who studied her with an inquisitive eye.

Opening the cash register, Mr. Byler slid a sheet of paper beneath the drawer. "How well do you know that young man?"

"Not well at all."

He peered at her over the top of his glasses. "Were you with Lydia on Saturday night?"

She avoided eye contact by straightening bins of carabiner hooks and lip balm on the counter. She had to come up with an answer—the right answer—fast. "I was with her, but we parted ways before midnight."

His shoulders slouched. "I fear she is mixed up in the wrong crowd."

With a quick glance, she checked the storefront windows.

Dustin had disappeared onto the crowded street. "Lydia's a smart girl."

But not when she partied. The half-truth caused her to cringe.

"I pray her mother and I make it through her *Rumspringa*, but you didn't hear me say that." He rubbed the back of his neck. "Oh, yes. Mrs. Byler wanted to celebrate your birthday with you. She baked cupcakes to share with the morning shift."

"How sweet of her to think of me."

"You may work for me, but we do love you like a daughter." He patted her shoulder. "I have orders to place. I'll be in my office if you need me."

"*Danke*." She stood taller and adjusted her apron.

Disappointing Mr. Byler was not an option, and she would die if anything jeopardized her job at his store. She would not cover for his daughter again.

CHAPTER THREE

Seated in the buggy beside Josiah, Mariah closed her cardigan against the wind as the horse cantered down the gravel drive past the Bylers' property to the acreage owned and maintained by her family for five generations. Wedged between the trees and a few low, dark clouds along the horizon, the sun's rays streaked the sky with shades of pink, reminding her of the cotton candy he'd bought for her this past summer at the Holmes County Fair.

"Bowling was fun." She crossed her legs.

"Great turnout."

"I'm glad your sister's boyfriend could join us. Seemed like she couldn't wait to see him."

"His cousin's visiting their family in Sugarcreek, so he got a break from the farm." Josiah steered the buggy up to the front porch. "Will you be in town tomorrow?"

"No. Since I picked up some extra hours for Lydia this week at the hardware store, I have chores to catch up on around here."

"Guess I'll see you at church on Sunday." He paused.

"Maybe we could go for a ride after lunch? As friends."

The setting sun cast an orange glow on his face, accentuating the color of his eyes, which reminded her of the Gulf's deep blue waters featured on the postcards that her three older sisters mailed home from Pinecraft in the winter.

"I'd like that *verra* much." Warmth rushed to her cheeks. "I appreciate you giving me a ride home."

"May I also take you to the singing? Again, as friends." he asked. "Unless you think you'd grow sick of me."

"I don't think that could ever happen."

"Wait there." A smile spread across his face, stretching the scar he got the day Buster died. Though his face hadn't changed much since his wounds had healed, the handsome man beside her was no longer the young boy she'd defended in the schoolyard. Racing around the buggy, he helped her step to the ground. "Until then." He held onto her hand longer than usual and rubbed his thumb across the back of her fingers. "I'll be lookin' forward to it."

An unfamiliar flutter caused her heart to beat faster. "Me too."

As she climbed the front porch steps, the sound of hooves in a trot reached her ears. She waited to open the door until his buggy disappeared down the lane.

"Psst...Mariah." The hushed voice came from the bushes to her left.

She jumped and peeked around a railing post. "Who's there?"

"It's me."

"Lydia? What are you doing?"

Her best friend emerged from the shadows dressed in jeans and an off-the-shoulder black top. "Come with me to the party tonight. It's gonna be *legendary*."

"So I've heard." Mariah rolled her eyes and ignored the puzzled look that crossed her friend's face.

"Then you'll come?"

"I won't. I'm exhausted from working extra hours *for you*, and I have many chores to do in the morning."

"Please come. You'll know a lot of people."

Mariah pictured their friends who had stumbled through the field the previous weekend, spilling the contents of their cups on those around them. Great. That was not helping Lydia's case.

"We'll just stay a short time. I'll leave when you're ready. Promise." She clenched her hands near her chest.

"*How 'bout you promise not to go to any more of those parties—unless escorted by me?*" Josiah's words played on a reel in her mind.

"Dustin and his friends are grilling, and we're roasting marshmallows."

She bit her lip. Dustin had said he hoped she'd be there.

Lydia extended her arms toward the deep blue sky. "And it's a beautiful night."

Mariah tilted her head back and spied the first star, which winked as if to say her secret was safe. She shifted her weight and fiddled with the edge of her sweater. "I can't believe I'm saying this, but you are right. This is my chance to run around before I join the church. Promise we won't stay out late?"

"You have my word."

"Fine. I'll go."

"Oh, thank you, thank you! You won't regret this. Do you still have my jeans from last weekend?"

"They're in my room." She glanced down the length of the front porch. The propane light in the kitchen still burned, but at this hour, her parents were sound asleep. She could tip-toe through the house, grab the jeans and a sweater, and sneak back outside without disturbing them. "I'll be back in a minute."

As she felt her way through the darkness, she ran into the corner of the grandfather clock and then jammed her toe on the baseboard. Leaning against the wall, she rubbed her sore foot. What was she doing? Sneaking out of the house to go to a party?

She should tell Lydia she'd changed her mind.

But when would she otherwise have this opportunity? Lydia *had* promised not to stay out too late.

Now or never.

Mariah grabbed the garments from under her bed and slipped back out the front door. "Let's go before I change my mind."

"Great. Follow me."

Sprinting down the lane toward the main road to catch up, Mariah soon settled into pace with her best friend. "How are we getting there?"

Lydia slowed to a brisk walk. "Dustin should be here any minute."

"Not on his motorcycle, I hope."

"No. His truck. We wouldn't all fit on the bike. Sometimes I wonder about you."

"I know. I'm nervous." She peeked around the bushes at the end of the driveway. "It's too dark for the Millers to see me through their binoculars, right?"

"The neighbors aren't spying on us. Well, I doubt they're on watch tonight." She shook her head. "Too many questions. Change your clothes behind those trees so you're hidden from headlights."

"Okay, okay. Will you hold my purse?" Mariah passed the handbag to her friend and ducked around the tree line.

"He's driving a few others to the party. I imagine you'll sit with them in the back. It might be chilly, but we're not going far. I'm sure someone will offer to keep you warm." The wind carried Lydia's whispers between the trees.

As Mariah slipped the bright pink sweater over her head, she remembered a story Josiah told her a few years ago about a group of English teens who were out riding around early one morning after a night of partying. While driving at high speeds, they miscalculated the bend in the road at the edge of the Weaver property. Josiah and his brother were in the barn milking the cows and feeding the horses when they heard the tires squeal. He claims he spared her the goriest details, but she grimaced as she recalled the mental images of the scene created in her imagination.

"You know, I'm really tired." She slipped her other arm into the sleeve. "Maybe this isn't such a *gut*—"

A diesel engine rumbled in the distance. "There they are! Hurry up!" Twin beams of light sliced through the darkness. Lydia combed her hair with her fingers and straightened her top to reveal her navel.

Mariah pulled her sweater down over her hips. This was her last chance to turn around and head home.

Gravel crunched as the F-150 slowed to a stop. Dustin cracked the driver's side door and the cab light cast a bright glow into the darkness.

"Well, well. Look who we have here." He stepped close to the girls. Lydia embraced him around his neck and lifted her feet off the ground. He held her with one arm and turned to Mariah, running a finger along her forearm with his free hand. She could smell beer on his breath, causing the butter-flies in her stomach to stir from hibernation. She shouldn't be doing this, especially since he'd been drinking. Pulling her arm away from his touch, she fished through her purse for a piece of gum.

"There's room back here." A deep voice called from the truck bed. The shadows separated, providing space for her.

"Come on. Jump in." A higher pitched voice urged from the blackness.

"Let's go. I'm ready to party." Lydia climbed into the cab.

Dustin touched her hand. "I'm glad you decided to come. It wouldn't be the same without you. If I'd known, I would've saved a seat for you up front."

It wouldn't be the same without you. She attempted to wipe the blush from her cheek on her sleeve. A nervous giggle escaped.

He nodded at the truck bed. "Need a lift?"

"No. I can manage." She hoisted herself into the seat created for her by the others. What would Josiah think about this? What about her parents? As she said a quick prayer, Dustin climbed into the cab and hit the gas pedal. Her body jolted to the right and she fell into the strong arms attached to the faceless body seated beside her.

"Hello." His voice was soft and smoky, and his breath smelled like the whiskey her mother had her sip when she had a bad cough—spicy and sweet. "Get ready to have the best night of your life."

CHAPTER FOUR

The pickup veered off the main drag and ventured down a dirt path through a field of soybeans. Those in the back of the truck with Mariah cheered. Someone played music through a cell phone, and the guy with the smoky voice began to sing. She filled her lungs with the chilly air and relaxed against the truck bed, bobbing her head to the familiar tune. As they passed by an Amish farm, the guy beside her whipped a rock at a mailbox illuminated by the truck's lights without missing a note.

She gasped.

Dustin slammed on his brakes. The truck slid to a stop on the side of the road, and he jumped from the driver's seat. "Who did that?"

"Me." The guy sat taller and squared his shoulders. "What's the big deal anyway?"

"Dude." He grabbed the guy's shirt collar and pulled his face close. "Not in my truck. Ever." Tilting his head toward her, Dustin placed his hand on her shoulder. "Show some respect." He bent down and whispered in her ear. "You okay?"

She stared straight ahead as her stomach churned, unable to offer an answer. Members of her church had been victims to the English teens who chose to sling rocks and bricks at homes and buggies before their cars raced off into the darkness. A few years ago, Josiah's brother suffered a broken arm when a rock ricocheted off the buggy's windshield. She took a deep breath and said a prayer.

Dustin rubbed her shoulder and then returned to his seat behind the wheel. After they rounded one more corner, the pickup rolled to a stop. The guy beside her jumped to the ground, grabbed her hand, and lifted her from the truck bed. When her feet were planted in the dirt, she turned to search for Lydia, but the guy didn't let go. Instead, he twirled her around and spun her into his arms. She swayed to the music with him.

"Girl, you've got no rhythm." He shouted over the music.

"Maybe I don't want to dance with you."

"Whatever." He dropped her hands and strutted toward the bonfire. A log cracked and embers shot into the night like fireworks.

Lydia appeared beside Mariah and put an arm around her shoulders. "How was the ride?"

"I'm not so sure about this—"

"Here." Her friend thrust a red plastic cup in her hand, splashing beer onto the hay beneath their feet.

Glancing from her hand to her friend, Mariah cocked her head to the side. "How'd
you—?"

"Never mind."

"But who gave it to you? What's in this?"

"Just drink it. It'll help you relax. Have some fun." A new song blared through the speakers, and Lydia danced toward the bonfire.

Dustin made eye contact with her from his post near the grills, where a group of guys stoked the coals and ripped open packages of hot dogs. "Let me know when you need a refill."

"*Dank*—thank you." She glanced into the cup and took a reluctant sip. Her eyes flicked through the growing crowd, estimating there to be at least a couple hundred teens—twice as many as filled the field at the last party. She spotted Lydia in the arms of another muscular *Englisher*. His hips were pressed against her backside, and they moved together to the beat. The heat rose to her cheeks, and she averted her eyes.

Sensing someone's presence, she turned around.

"I see you watching them dance." Dustin removed the cup from her hands, took a sip, and then set it aside, stepping behind her. "I'm glad you're here. Let's show 'em how it's done." With a sure grip, he placed his hands on her hips and linked his index fingers in her belt loops. He pulled her close and rocked back and forth. His shirt smelled of campfire, and the musky scent of his cologne wasn't as offensive as it had been the last time. She closed her eyes and took in a deep breath. Leaning her head on his shoulder, she permitted him to guide her movements with his body. A warmth consumed her from the top of her head to her toes. For a second, she didn't want the song to end—didn't want him to let go.

"This is nice," he whispered in her ear.

"Mm-hmm," she sighed.

"Hey, Dustin. Need you for a sec." The voice rang out from behind the grills.

"Man." He blew out his breath and turned to her. "Don't go anywhere, 'kay?"

Mariah smiled. She reached for her cup and took a long swig. This wasn't so bad after all. Could she get used to this?

Cars filled with rowdy teens continued to pull into the field. The music got louder, and the faces blurred. Lydia had disappeared, and Mariah forgot about the time, her chores, and Josiah's request. Dustin had spent a majority of the evening by her side, and his advances tonight did not offend her. Maybe it was the beer? Maybe there was something happening between them?

He gathered her limp body into his arms as another song blasted through the speakers, and they moved in sync without much effort.

"Time to break it up." A man's authoritative voice boomed over the music, and the beats stopped. Without additional warning, police officers emerged from a dozen squad cars and marched into the field with flashlights.

"Police! Break it up!"

Cups dropped. Kids screamed and sprinted further into the field toward the trees. Dustin shoved her aside. Tires squealed.

Mariah fought to focus ahead. A clean-cut man wandered through the crowd. Though he wore dark jeans and a charcoal gray sweatshirt with "The North Face" printed in orange block letters across the chest, he appeared to be older than the others around them. He swung the beam of a flashlight in her face—she stood frozen in the spotlight. Fishing around in his back pocket, he pulled out a pad of paper and flashed his badge. "What's your name, miss?" He held a pen above the notepad.

She stared at the gun holster on his hip and burst into tears.

He bent near her and sniffed. "Have you been drinking?" His stern tone caused her to tremble.

She nodded and stretched the hem of her sweater over her

hips.

"I'm gonna need to see your ID."

"I'm Amish, sir. I turned 18 last week, but I don't have a driver's license nor an ID card yet. I might have my library card with me." She opened the bag she carried.

"No need." His low laugh carried in the wind.

She failed to see what he found to be so humorous. Tremors shook her body.

"Your name."

"M-Mariah Mast, sir."

He studied her face. "Ah, are you related to the Masts who own the bakery in town?"

"Yes," she whispered. The mention of her family made her feel nauseous.

"Contrary to popular belief, I don't go in there for the donuts." His expression brightened, and he laughed. "Great coffee though." He leaned close and tilted his chin down, glaring at her from beneath his thick brows. "I didn't *see* you drinking or even holding a cup. I'll be giving you a warning—this time."

She surveyed the faces in the crowd. Where was Dustin? Lydia? How would she get home?

"Oh no." She groaned as the field spun around her. She pulled her hair over her shoulder and buried her face in her hands.

"What's wrong? Friends ditch you? Don't worry, young lady. I'll make sure you get home safe and sound. Come with me." He took her by the elbow and led her to his squad car. The bright flashes of red and blue light made her head throb. She swallowed hard to avoid throwing up.

Numb, she stared out the window. She should never have allowed Lydia to talk her into this. Her older sisters didn't run with a group who partied during their *Rumspringa*. How would her parents react to her sneaking out? How would they respond when she arrived home in a police car? Would they smell beer on her breath?

Terror seized her thoughts—Josiah.

CHAPTER FIVE

Though the muscles between her shoulder blades burned, Mariah dared not shift on the wooden bench. She'd sat still for over two and a half hours. The church service would soon end. Until then, she'd maintain perfect posture.

By now, everyone in the community seemed to know about her involvement with the police at the party. They wore their disappointment on their faces, and she couldn't bear the thought that those she cared about disapproved of her actions.

Grateful her mother and grandmother received her with open arms when the police cruiser pulled up to her home, she closed her eyes against the image of her father, standing in the driveway at that late hour, rubbing the back of his neck. Earlier this morning, he stood in the same spot with Mr. Byler, their heads lowered. Perhaps their neighbor could convince him to forgive her like he had five years ago, when she'd chosen the hardware store over the bakery. She couldn't endure another six-month silent treatment.

Before the church service began, her father stood beside

Mr. Byler, talking with the other men outside the barn. She hung her head and hustled past them on the way to her seat.

Aware of Josiah's stare from across the aisle throughout the morning, she managed to avoid eye contact. But she couldn't dodge an interaction with him forever—an awkward conversation was inevitable. She prayed, asking God to go before her on this blessed day, to give her words when she spoke with him.

When they finished singing the final hymn, family and friends worked together to transform the Schrocks' barn into a dining hall. Josiah and his friends rearranged the long wooden benches that served as seats and tables in the empty space now free of tools, farm equipment, and animals set out to pasture earlier in the week. Girls with goldenrod hair set out the tableware and napkins while two small sisters set bowls of pickled beets on tables. Women dressed in shades of burnt rust, plum, and mulberry brought out platters of pretzels, breads, lunchmeats, and cheeses and placed them on the table at Mrs. Schrock's direction.

Since Mrs. Schrock had been ill, her family offered to bring sweet treats to share. Mariah didn't like the idea of working in the bakery—this was no secret, but she enjoyed baking with her grandmother, mother, and sisters at home. Throughout the week, they had gathered in the modest kitchen in the *dawdihouse* to mix cookie batters and roll out pastry dough for pie crusts by hand. She had worked hard to establish her role in the family kitchen, and helping a neighbor in need filled her soul.

Mariah hurried to the house to grab the basket of mason jars filled with peanut butter spread she'd prepared. She returned to the barn, where the smell of smoked ham and turkey slices caused her belly to grumble.

As she arranged the basket in the center of the dessert table, footsteps approached—the cadence familiar. She held her breath.

"Mariah? Can we talk?" Josiah's voice dissipated her hunger.

She focused on the dessert table, rearranging the mason jars in the basket. This conversation could not happen here in front of everyone. "I'm busy."

"It's important."

"So is this. And I have to help pour coffee for the men."

"Please?"

"We should go outside, but I don't have my coat. Can't this wait?"

"What I have to say won't take long." He extended his arm as if to say he'd follow her lead.

Biting her lip, she took cautious steps into the sunlight. She squinted as she surveyed the yard for a spot away from the barn and curious eavesdroppers who awaited their shift to eat with hungry bellies. A grove of magnolia trees, which stood beyond the rows of buggies at the edge of the yard, would shelter them from the bitter breeze. "Let's sit on the swing. Is that okay?"

"Whatever you'd like."

His tone caused her to cringe, but she sat and placed her hands in her lap. Thankful the church wagon blocked them from the view of onlookers, she picked her fingernails while the silence hung between them, thick like the peanut butter spread.

He exhaled through his nose. "I don't want to ask you this, but I have to know. Had you already planned to go to that party when I dropped you off after bowling?"

"What? No." She braced her hands on her thighs and

turned to face him. "I watched your buggy all the way down the lane, and Lydia caught me before I went inside the house."

He huffed and set his lips in a thin line. "Were you with the same guy you hung out with last weekend?"

"His name is Dustin."

"Mariah." He hung his head. "I thought you promised not to go to another party in the field unless we went together?"

"I never made that promise." Deep pain flashed in his blue eyes, and she regretted blurting the words.

She focused on a buggy rolling along the road near the horizon. "Look, you're one of my dearest friends, and I don't want to hurt you. But if I'm being honest, I've been having doubts about my future. This is my chance to figure out how I want to live the rest of my life."

"No thanks to your new English *friends*." His nostrils flared.

"No. I've been feeling this way for several months—before I met them. Now that I have met them, who knows? Maybe I will choose to get baptized into the church. Maybe I won't."

"You've had doubts about getting baptized?"

"Not necessarily. But I wonder if maybe *Gott* has other plans for me. I'm 18 years old, and I'm being asked to make a *huge* decision that will affect the rest of my life."

"Our lives," he muttered. "Do you know how hard I've—" He ripped off his hat and kicked a pebble into the grass. "And on top of everything else. I can't believe this—after all I've done for us, for our future."

"I need time—"

"Well, guess what, Mariah. I can't *promise* I'll still be waiting for you when you finally figure it out." The veins in his neck bulged, and his cheeks turned red. He rose from the swing and stomped away.

"Josiah. Wait!" She jumped to her feet, and the swing slammed into the back of her legs.

He veered toward the barn without giving her a second glance, which proved to be more painful than the sting in her calves.

"Why doesn't he understand I need time to figure out who I am and who *Gott* wants me to be?" she whispered.

Gritting her teeth, she swallowed her tears and returned to the barn, determined to do what her family expected of her—to face the consequences of her actions. Despite the hushed conversations and sideways glances in her direction, she stood tall and forced a smile as she poured black coffee into white plastic mugs. But once lunch had been cleaned up, she rode the two miles home alongside her family without speaking a word, ran into the house and down the hall, and plopped face-first onto her bed. Only then did she allow the tears to fall.

When she emerged from her bedroom, exhausted and ready for a snack, she found her grandmother sitting at the kitchen table, reading a newspaper, and sipping a cup of coffee. She had removed the black apron she had worn to church, and her burgundy dress enhanced the rosy glow to her complexion. Mariah sliced a piece of cake she didn't have the taste for at lunch. She slid into the chair next to her grandmother and poked the buttercream with a fork.

Grandma reached over and placed her palm between her shoulder blades, rubbing her hand in a circle. "You look like you're having a rough day, my sweet child."

"I knew my actions on Friday would disappoint people, but I did it anyway. Josiah and I had a conversation about the other night. I've caused him a great deal of pain." She savored a bite of dark chocolate—a welcome relief from the bitter taste of bile she'd been dealing with all weekend.

"*Rumspringa* is a time to explore and experiment. You're collecting information to help you make a decision that will affect the rest of your life. This is a big deal."

"That's what I told *Daed* and Josiah. I feel like I need time to figure out who I am and who *Gott* wants me to be. Nobody else seems to understand." Tears moistened her eyes again.

"Oh, I do." She clasped her hands to her chest. "You sound like me when I was your age."

"I do?"

"Have I ever told you the story of my *Rumspringa*?"

"No." Mariah drew out the word.

"When I was your age, I caused a big stir in our community. The bishop wasn't happy with me." She swiped a dollop of frosting from the plate, and then plopped the sugary bite in her mouth and smiled—a twinkle in her eye.

"What did you do?"

Voices echoed in the hallway, and the volume of chatter grew louder.

"Well—" her grandmother leaned close and lowered her voice. "We won't be alone for long, so for now, I'll tell you the bishop was an uncle to the boy I was *supposed* to marry."

Mariah dropped her fork.

CHAPTER SIX

Lydia smacked her lips.

"Stop licking your fingers. That's gross." Mariah dried her hands on a dishtowel and slung it over her shoulder.

"Can't help it. This is the best I've ever tasted."

Scraping the side of the mixing bowl, Mariah filled the final mason jar with Monkey Butter. "I think it's better this time because we used ground coconut instead of flakes. Better texture." She smiled at her best friend and then licked the spatula.

"Hey!" Lydia slipped her hand into an oven mitt, grabbed a hot jar, and placed it on the counter near the open window. "I have not spent my entire Saturday with you in this kitchen for noth—"

Glass shattered, and the sticky mixture of bananas and pineapple oozed onto the countertop.

"Oh no! Lydia, what are you thinking? We need to let the jars cool first." Mariah used tongs to remove another jar from the boiling water bath. She placed it on a dish towel spread on the counter away from the open window and the chilly breeze that fluttered the kitchen curtains.

"Oops." Lydia twirled. "I may look good in an apron, but you know I'm not gifted in the kitchen."

Mariah grabbed a loaf of white bread from the baker's rack and hit her best friend with it. "This has nothing to do with being gifted in the kitchen and you know it."

With quick footwork, Lydia ran to the other side of the room, and the long wooden dining table stretched between them. Mariah ran her fingers over the words "I love you"— words pressed into the plank by her years ago—a little six-year-old crafting Mother's Day cards for her relatives. That was the first year her grandmother had asked her to help with the seasonal canning. The following year, Lydia accepted the invitation to join them. After taking part in the tradition for over a decade, how could the girl be so helpless in the kitchen?

Though her best friend spent many Saturday afternoons with Mariah, canning favorites like three bean salad and homemade applesauce, Lydia never returned home and practiced preparing the Mast-family recipes she learned. It didn't help that she and Mrs. Byler were the only women in the house either. Her mother had married Mr. Byler and moved to Holmes County, leaving her family in Shipshewana, Indiana. As Mariah knelt beside Lydia to pick up pieces of the broken jar, she held her tongue.

With the shards of glass in the garbage, and the gooey mess cleaned from the counter, they escaped the hot kitchen by taking a break on the front porch.

"Do you have plans tonight?" Lydia asked from the swing.

"I think I'm going to turn in early." Mariah lowered, choosing to sit on the stairs. "I keep saying I should stop reading those romance novels of yours, but I can't put this one down. I have about a third left."

"Are you still on the second book in the series?"

Mariah nodded.

"Let me know when you finish. You are not going to believe who she chooses in the end."

She jammed fingers in her ears. "Don't tell me!"

"I'll run the third book over to you. Once you finish book two, you're gonna want to start the next one immediately. Trust me."

"That's okay. You can give it to me at church."

Lydia's eyes widened. "In that case, you'll want to wait to finish it. I'm telling you. And that means you're free to come with me to a party tonight."

Mariah waved her hands. "No way."

"Dustin and his friends will be there," she said in a sing-song voice.

"Absolutely not. I may trust your choice in books, but I'm not falling for that again."

"Falling for what?" Her best friend batted long eyelashes.

"Your moves don't work on me. In fact, I'm still a little mad at you for leaving me in that field."

"That was like a month ago. And I thought you said you forgave me."

"I did, but that doesn't mean I've not learned from the mistakes I made that night. Going to those parties isn't my idea of fun."

"Dustin's been asking about you."

A diesel engine rumbled in the distance.

"I'm not going with you." Mariah shifted on the porch step. "Please don't say his name again."

—

A gust of wind swirled the dusting of snow around her feet

while Mariah held the ladder, allowing Mr. Byler to adjust the greenery above the store's front door. The fringe on her scarf tickled her cheek, though she didn't dare let her mittened hands relax their grip on the metal legs.

In a few short minutes, customers would take advantage of the extended hours of operation and bustle through the aisles in search of last-minute decorations and Christmas gifts for those hard-to-buy-for loved ones.

The store owner removed a green zip tie from his teeth and fastened the evergreen swag to the store sign above the door. "There. That should do the trick." He climbed down the ladder. "Thank you for all your help this season, Mariah. I've come to really count on you."

"My pleasure. I know I let you down earlier in the fall, and I'm glad you allowed me to keep my job. I've learned a lot working here, and my family appreciates the extra money each week."

"Extra money is a blessing, especially around the holidays." He folded the ladder and carried it inside the store. "You will join our family for breakfast on Christmas Eve again this year, won't ya?" he asked over his shoulder.

"Of course. I wouldn't miss it." She smiled and ordered the magazines and candy bars near the register. "Do you need help with anything else, or shall I prepare to open for the day?"

"We're all set." He disappeared into the stockroom.

As she touched the car and truck magazine Dustin had flipped through weeks ago, the sleigh bells on the door jangled.

"Welcome to Byler's." Shaking away the handsome memory, she turned to greet her first customer.

Dustin? Heat rushed to her cheeks as if he could know her

thoughts.

He straightened his spine as he approached the register. "Hey, pretty girl. It's good to see you."

"Hi." She avoided his eyes which proved to be a mistake. Why did he have to look so good? Those shoulders. His hands.

No. He left her alone in the field. She squirted cleaner on the counter and wiped it dry with a towel.

"I'm so glad I've finally run into you," he said. "I've felt terrible since well, you know—I stopped in a few times after that, but you weren't here."

"Really?" She squinted. "I've worked a lot over this holiday season. If that's the truth, I'm surprised we didn't cross paths."

His steps brought him closer to the counter, where they stood a couple of feet apart. "I'm sorry for leaving you. I mean it. I don't know what I was thinking. I made a mistake."

"A police officer had to drive me home."

"Are you kidding?" His mouth fell open. "I had no idea. I thought you followed me. When I couldn't find you, I figured you found a ride home with a friend."

"Well, now you know." She organized a stack of collection envelopes for a local charity.

The sleigh bells jingled.

She faced the front of the store as a mother shuffled her toddler through the door. "Welcome to Byler's. I'll be with you in a moment." She turned back to Dustin. "Is there something I can help you with? I have to get to work."

"One more minute, Mariah. Please. I—I'm sorry. I truly am sorry. Do you forgive me?"

"Forgive you? Well—" she tilted her head. "Of course I forgive you."

His strong shoulders lowered and the lines in his forehead relaxed. "I've missed seeing you around."

He'd missed her? Lydia hadn't been bending the truth. Mariah bit her lip to conceal a smile as it threatened to spread across her face.

"Let me make it up to you." He hit her arm with a playful touch. "Maybe we can grab a hot chocolate?"

He'd missed her *and* he wanted to spend time together? Had she been wrong about him after all?

"Excuse me. Oh, Merry Christmas, Mr. Verona." Mr. Byler tipped a file folder in his direction. "I hope your parents are well."

"They are."

"Good to hear. Mariah, when you're finished helping him, I could use a hand over in ornaments."

"I'll be right there."

"Go ahead." Dustin grinned, revealing a crooked upper tooth. "I'll drop back in later to see if you're free."

"See you then." He'd return soon, and they'd set a time to get together. Nerves and expectation fought for space in the chambers of her heart.

"Mr. Byler, sir?" Dustin followed her boss toward the ornament aisle and produced a paper from inside his coat. "Could I hang this flyer on your bulletin board?"

Her boss read over the paper and nodded. "I'll be sure our family stops in to show our support."

As Mariah strained to eavesdrop, the woman with the toddler emptied her purse on the counter. "Now, where did I put my wallet? Oh, it's in the car. Had to have my coffee this morning. Come here, Timmy." She plopped the boy on the counter. "Watch him for me for a minute, would ya? Mommy'll be right back." The woman dashed through the door before Mariah had a chance to answer.

"Um, okay?" She glanced around the store to see if there were other witnesses to this chaos. "Hi, Timmy."

The little boy screamed. Alligator tears streaked his cheeks as she picked him up.

Dustin appeared beside her and patted the boy's back. "Try singing 'Rudolph, the Red-Nosed Reindeer.'"

As the lyrics squeaked from her throat, she bounced the toddler on her hip. He quieted and stared at her with round, wet eyes.

"How'd you know that would work?" she asked.

Dustin raised his eyebrows. "I didn't. You're a natural. Have fun. I'll see you later." He slapped the counter on his way out of the store.

Pausing mid-bounce, she stared at the child. "What do you think about that?" She poked his nose with her finger. When the boy stuck out his bottom lip, she mirrored his expression. "Such a pitiful face you're making." His eyes filled until she resumed the song. The red mittens clipped to the sleeves of his jacket swung back and forth as he clapped.

His mother raced through the open doorway, the last leaves of the season swirling behind her. She bumped into a wreath display and dropped her wallet on the ground. Without looking up, she asked, "How much do I owe you?"

Mariah set the boy on the counter. "For what, ma'am?"

"Oh, Timmy." She took a few steps and bent to pick up a red stocking from the floor. "This." She slammed it on the counter. "New puppy chewed up his other one. Wouldn't be Christmas without hanging stockings by the fire." She rolled her eyes.

Mariah decided this woman wouldn't want to hear about Amish Christmas customs, so she remained quiet. "Fifteen twenty-five."

The mother handed her a gold credit card.

"Oh, we don't accept that credit card. Any others are fine, though."

"Of course you don't." Her voice dripped with irritation as she rifled through the stack of cards in her wallet. "Here you go." She clicked a button on her phone. "We're late."

"Would you please sign here?" Mariah slid the receipt and a pen across the counter.

After scribbling her name on the slip of paper, the lady scooped up the little boy and snatched the stocking. "Let's go."

She hadn't even said thank you. Why did people tend to forget their manners around the holidays?

As the mother hurried out the door, the toddler watched Mariah. He opened and shut his hand. "Bye. Bye."

Mariah waved. "Merry Christmas, little guy."

The boxes of both white and colored Christmas lights needed to be straightened on the shelves. On her way to that aisle, Mariah wandered past the bulletin board, and Dustin's flyer caught her eye. *Spaghetti Benefit Dinner. This Friday. 5pm to 7pm. St. Francis UMC. All proceeds will purchase toys and clothes for needy children.*

Though she'd been angry with him for weeks, he had searched for her to apologize. He helped her calm the little boy. And he served others through his church. Maybe she had judged him too quickly.

CHAPTER SEVEN

Mariah hung her apron on the hook near the register, then slid her arms into the sleeves of her gray wool coat and tied a black bonnet over her *kapp*.

With a skip in her step, she wiggled her fingers into her gloves and headed toward the coffee shop on the corner. Dustin had looked so handsome when he stopped by during her lunch break. Had her answer to meet when her shift ended come too quickly?

Passing by the coffee shop's picture window, she spotted him seated at a booth in the corner. He waved, and she stepped into the cozy building decorated with bumblebees and black gingham.

"There she is." He stood, his eyes twinkled. Her frozen fingertips tingled.

"Have you been waiting long?" She slid into the booth as he returned to his seat.

"Nope. Just got here. I missed lunch. Are you hungry?"

"No. I'm gonna get hot chocolate." She removed her gloves and scarf and stripped off her coat.

He flipped the menu over and perused the other side.

"Speaking of food, I wanted to ask you about the flyer you hung up in the store today."

"Yeah. For the spaghetti dinner." He paused as the waitress, wearing a black apron embroidered with the café's logo, placed two glasses of water on the table.

"Welcome." The woman pulled a pad of paper from her apron pocket. "Are you ready to order, or do you need another minute or two?"

"We're ready." Dustin motioned for Mariah to go first, and he leaned back in the booth.

With orders placed, he said, "Yeah, so I don't know much about the spaghetti dinner. The girl I've been seeing attends that church. I told her I'd hang a few flyers up around town."

"The girl you've been seeing?" Mariah gasped when she realized she'd uttered the words aloud.

The waitress paused next to the table and drew a straw from her apron pocket, which she set next to a soda for Dustin. The bubbles of carbonation in his glass bounced to the surface before bursting. Much like her heart.

"This plate is hot." Another server placed his order in front of him. "And here's your hot cocoa. Perfect choice on a day like today."

"Perfect choice alright." Mariah repeated without moving her lips. As she stirred the creamy beverage, steam escaped from the mug. She needed a way to escape this situation.

"Her name's Julie." He sprinkled oyster crackers in his bowl. "You'd really like her. I met her about a week after I last saw you. I'm glad you agreed to get together. I wanted to make up for leaving you behind."

Mariah took a sip from her mug and tried to relax. She had misunderstood his intentions. It wasn't his fault. Or was it?

Why did she continue to trust this guy when she got hurt every single time she was with him? She pretended to pay attention, nodding now and again as he talked about himself nonstop, until she'd reached the bottom of her mug. By this point, he had barely made a dent in his meal.

She flicked her eyes to a clock hanging near the kitchen. "Excuse me. It's getting late. I'd better get home now." She slid a five-dollar bill across the table to him. "This should be enough to cover my drink. Thank you for the invitation."

"What? You have to go—already?" He wiped chili grease from his fingers with a napkin.

She collected her belongings and stood.

"Wait." His fingertips brushed her forearm. "I can drive you home."

Pulling her arm away, she took a deep breath. "You know, you apologized for the party. As far as I'm concerned, we're *gut*." Heat rushed to her cheeks. "I hope you and Julie are happy together." She charged out of the coffee shop without giving him a chance to respond.

Wrestling the wind, she wrapped the warm wool coat around her body. Huge snowflakes fell heavy around her, a half an inch of fresh powder covered the roads. Laughter echoed in her ears. She stepped aside to allow a group of ladies—armed with shopping bags and carry-out containers—pass her on the sidewalk. Instead of following the tourists, she lifted the hem of her dress and stepped over the bank of snow onto the street. At least the long walk would give her time to collect her thoughts.

Had she truly believed a relationship with Dustin could have worked? At times, she convinced her heart that the worlds in which they lived didn't matter as much as the feelings they felt for each other. But those fantasies only happened in the pages of romance novels. She should stop reading them—stop filling her head with nonsense.

At this time of evening, with a cloudless sky, the sun would sit low on the horizon. The bakery had closed for the day. By choosing to meet Dustin after work, she had missed her ride home. The tips of her ears began to burn as anger crept into her thoughts.

How could she have been so foolish? She'd disappointed her family once when she hadn't wanted to work at the bakery. She'd disappointed them a second time by sneaking out to a party and then getting a police escort home. How would she explain why she was cold and wet and late to help prepare dinner?

Salty tears spilled, stinging her chapped cheeks as she prayed for guidance. A horse's hooves pounded the pavement, and a buggy slowed to a stop beside her. She blotted her face with her gloves.

"Mariah?" Josiah's voice caused new tears to flow. "How long have you been out here? The weather is terrible. Get in. I'll take you home." He offered her his hand.

Climbing into the buggy, she welcomed the break from the blustery wind.

"You're crying."

"I'm fine." She sniffled.

"Why didn't you ride home with your family? Are you okay?"

She wriggled into a different position. "I don't want to talk about it. I appreciate the ride."

He unfolded the blanket, which laid across his lap, and spread it over her legs.

"Why, Josiah? Why are you nice to me? I've hurt you over

and over, and I've caused you a lot of pain." She choked out a sob and covered her face with her hands. "I don't deserve your friendship."

"Come now. Don't talk like that. Would you like a tissue?" He reached for the travel pack in the buggy's storage compartment.

She dried her eyes. "Through it all, you continue to treat me with kindness."

"Of course I treat you with kindness. I love you. I've loved you for years."

And there he'd said it. With three words, he confirmed what she had believed to be true. What should she say? What could she say?

"I bet you're freezing." He cleared his throat. "I'm gonna get goin'. C'mon, Pete. Tch-tch." The Standardbred lifted his head and began to trot toward home.

With each gust of wind, she struggled to ignore her discomfort—both the physical and emotional. But the silence that stretched between them bothered her the most. Twice she started to say something—to ask him about his day, but the words froze on her vocal cords.

He steered the buggy down the drive to her family's property and turned his focus from the road to her. "I've kept my distance in recent weeks because I've been trying to give you the space you asked for to, you know, figure it all out."

With stiff fingers, she picked at a thread she had snagged on her glove while helping Mr. Byler rearrange an outdoor Christmas tree display—the task she'd finished before meeting Dustin. "I'm doing a great job figuring it out, that's for sure." Sarcasm laced her voice.

"Please know I'm here for you—even if you don't wanna talk."

She lowered her head. Oh how she desperately wanted him to stop the buggy and wrap her in his strong embrace. But instead, she took a deep breath and concentrated on the farmhouse. Kerosene lanterns glowed with warmth in the windows, and she longed for a hot shower.

"Before you go," he said. "I wanted to let you know I'm moving."

She jerked her head in his direction. "Moving?"

"To the house next door to us. Our neighbors are retiring—heading down south. They agreed to sell me their property—the house, the land, and that includes the alpaca farm."

The breath she'd been holding appeared as a cloud of fog. "*Wunderbaar*! I love alpacas."

"I know you do."

"I'm truly happy for you."

"It's been a bit of a mess—long story—almost didn't happen, but my brother helped me pull it off. I've been going through boxes in my closet, and I found the picture you drew of me and Buster. Remember?"

"How could I forget?" Hard to believe he'd kept it all this time. God had not blessed her with the gift of drawing.

"I'm gonna hang it in my new place."

"I thought the drawing might brighten your spirits. You were heartbroken when you discovered your cow had been sold to the butcher."

His shoulders slumped. "I watched that calf's birth, and my *daed* let me name him. Raised him on my own for two years."

"How old were we?"

"I was seven." He ran his thumb over the thick scar filling in the cleft of his chin—the scar from the tin bucket he'd thrown at his brother for teasing him about Buster—the tin bucket that ricocheted off Joshua's arm and into Josiah's face, knocking out his two front teeth. "You were six."

The distant look in his eye told her he had revisited those dark days. "You okay?"

"You mighta been tiny, but you got after the kids who teased me about my lisp. I knew back then I wanted to marry you someday."

"Josiah—"

"I'm sorry. We've been through a lot together. I miss you."

"I miss you too."

He reached over and grasped her hand in his. "Take care of yourself. Merry Christmas." His bright blue eyes twinkled like the Christmas lights strung across store rooftops in town.

"Merry Christmas," she said, her voice barely above a whisper. She climbed down from the buggy and rushed into the house. Though she should change into a dry dress and help in the kitchen, she instead collapsed onto her bed. She didn't care about getting the log cabin quilt damp with her wet clothes, nor her tears.

Despite her poor choices and her negative attitude toward Josiah, he said he loved her. But why? She didn't deserve his attention or his affection.

A knock on the bedroom door disturbed her thoughts.

"Come in," she called with a raspy voice.

The door creaked open, and her grandmother's rosy face appeared. "Dinner's ready."

"I'm not hungry." Mariah rolled over and peeled the layers of clothing from her sticky body in an effort to get comfortable.

"Oh, dear. Look at you." The wrinkles around her grandmother's eyes deepened.

"It's been a bad day." Mariah shivered.

"Does this have anything to do with that handsome *Englisher*?"

"Partly. How'd you know?"

"I stopped in the coffee shop to buy Mrs. Schrock a gift card, and I saw you sitting with him."

Turning her face away, Mariah shook her head. "I'm so embarrassed."

"Don't be." Grandma smoothed wisps of hair across her forehead. "I'm sorry you've had a bad day. Just remember a mistake here and there doesn't make you a bad person. How you react after making a mistake matters more than what you did."

CHAPTER EIGHT

After pulling on her boots and black bonnet, Mariah cinched her coat. A thin layer of ice crunched beneath her feet as she rushed through the snow to the barn. Tiny icicles clung to tree branches and glistened when woken by the first rays of the morning sun. Above her, the chimney spewed a gray plume that swirled into the gloomy sky. Her nose tingled and her eyes watered—from the cold, at least that's what she reckoned. She blinked away the painful memories associated with the smoky smell.

The heavy barn door creaked a good morning, but the groan that followed told her it would have preferred not to be disturbed. Once sheltered from the wind by the thick wooden walls, she wasted no time and got to work.

Grain spilled into the feed bins, and the goats pranced toward her like tap dancers, their hooves doing a series of shuffle ball changes against the concrete floor. While at the fair in August, Josiah led her to a stage where the Holmes County Dancers performed a routine to "Singing in the Rain." Their tapping toes and rainbow-colored umbrellas mesmerized her.

Though he had wanted to catch the beginning of the barrel races, he stood beside her until the dancers had finished. Smiling at the memory, she set down her bucket and attempted the basic step. To this day, she had never confided to anyone how she had searched for tap dancing video tutorials on the computer at work. Nor had she confessed that she'd practiced the moves while alone in her room.

The lowing of a cattle drew her to the tasks at hand. Crossing the barn to the stalls, she secured the first cow to the gate and then squatted on a stool near a full udder. She rubbed her palms together as she moved from one to the next, milking half a dozen cows by the light of an oil lantern.

After transferring the fresh milk from the bucket to a stainless steel can, she grabbed a basket from the storage closet and crossed the yard to the henhouse. Gold and orange bands striped the eastern sky, blurring through the fog that surrounded her with each breath. The morning's stillness invited her to appreciate the warm colors until a gust of wind covered her with bitter cold, causing her to ball her fists to work out the stiffness in her fingers.

With the basket of eggs in hand, she rushed back to the house and crept into the kitchen where the generator's gentle hum stirred her into action. The aroma of crispy bacon and the sound of sizzling sausage soon filled the kitchen. She shifted dishes in the cabinet and reached for a large mixing bowl. As she cracked the eggs, Grandma's slippers scuffed along the wooden floor.

"You're up early this morning." The older woman secured an apron over her mauve dress and poured a glass of orange juice.

"I couldn't sleep, so I headed outside and completed all the chores."

"All the chores?" Grandma's voice rose an octave.

"I haven't been around much this holiday season because I've been working all of those extra hours for Mr. Byler." She whisked the eggs with a fork. "Don't get me wrong, I love it. But I haven't pulled my weight around here for weeks."

"Oh, Sweetheart. You're always thinking of others." She tucked a stray lock of hair beneath her *kapp*.

Mariah pictured Josiah and chewed the inside of her cheek. "Not always, but thank you."

Guilt battled with shame to capture her thoughts. Would her grandmother figure out this extra effort at home and at work was her way to make up for the mistakes she'd made in the fall? Would the woman learn that her thoughts were more often self-centered than not?

Grandma rinsed her glass and then sidled up next to Mariah. "Here. Let me help you." After adding black pepper to the bowl, she poured the eggs into a casserole dish, added the sausage, and sprinkled cheese over the top. On her way to the oven, she leaned close to Mariah and whispered, "Since we're alone, maybe I could finish telling you the story of my *Rumspringa*."

They settled into seats next to each other at the kitchen table.

"*Gut matin.*" Her father stretched his arms overhead as he entered the kitchen. He stumbled through the room and smoothed his dark hair with a quick sweep of his hand. "Breakfast smells delicious. I'll eat before I head out to the barn."

"No need, John." Grandma patted her on the shoulder and then returned to the cutting board to slice oranges. "Mariah's already done the chores. And she helped make all this food."

"Mariah? You didn't have to—"

"Yes, I did." She wiped her hands on a dishtowel.

A sigh escaped his lips. He peeked in the oven. "Is that *Mammi* Mast's famous breakfast casserole?"

Mariah lowered her chin. "It's only famous in our family."

He popped a juicy slice of citrus fruit in his mouth, then hung his thumbs on his suspenders. "I wub it."

"John!" Grandma hit him with a dishtowel. "Don't talk with your mouth full. I raised you better than that."

As he stole another orange slice, her mother and sisters appeared with sleepy eyes. They wore dresses sewn from fabric the color of mistletoe.

"Merry Christmas," Mariah said as she carried silverware past them and into the dining room. A fresh set of quilted placemats covered the worn oak table at each seat. She had helped her mother choose the red and green Christmas Stars pattern, and the colors complemented the winter blooms displayed in a pair of vases on the buffet.

Her father followed and stopped beside the picture window that overlooked the land behind the Bylers' home. Clicking his tongue, he said, "That wind is mighty strong. The branches on these trees are bending under the weight from the snowstorm the other night. Think we're in for another couple of inches."

She placed the last fork on the table and peered outside as gusts of air rattled the windowpanes. Though their neighbors lived close, she'd want to grab her warmest sweater before she headed over to visit.

Her mouth watered as her mother walked by with cranberry muffins she had warmed in the oven. The rest of her family entered the room with arms loaded with casserole dishes, platters, and pitchers. As everyone settled around the table, Mariah glanced at the clock on the wall. Did she have enough time to enjoy a small plate? Maybe a couple bites of that sausage egg casserole?

A deafening crack followed by a thunderous boom shook the farmhouse on its foundation.

Her father jumped to his feet and spun toward the window. "The tree!"

The family filled in the spaces around him. Mariah ducked beneath her sister's elbow and peered into the neighbors' yard. "At least it fell away from the house."

"That sound!" Her mother covered her mouth with one hand and shook her head. "It could've been so much worse."

"Mariah," the deepness of her father's voice sounded over the chatter in the room. "When are you going next door to visit?"

"Soon."

"Let Samuel know I'll recruit the neighbors. We'll help him chop the firewood. If we can get enough volunteers, we can knock it out in two-three hours." He returned his focus to the fallen tree. "By God's grace, we have all been blessed."

—

Mariah opened the Bylers' front door without knocking and inhaled, filling her nostrils with pine-scented candles and the aroma of cinnamon rolls baking in the propane oven.

"Merry Christmas!" Lydia hurried through the hallway, her plum dress swinging around her legs, and greeted Mariah with a tight squeeze. "Let me take your coat. You can place the bags on the hearth." She motioned into the family room with an elbow. "I'll be another minute or two. I'm helping my mother finish in the kitchen."

"You? In the kitchen? I'll help. Let me set these down."

"Oh, stop." Lydia called over her shoulder. "*Daed*, Mariah's here!"

Mariah entered the family room and removed the reusable shopping bag from her shoulder. Mr. Byler appeared from the room across the hall and placed his mug of coffee on the table. Flames flickered in the fireplace and cast an orange glow on his bald head.

"Merry Christmas, my dear." He wrapped his arm around her and gave her a quick kiss on her *kapp*. "We're glad you could join us."

"I'm glad to be here."

"We prefer to stay busy during the holidays."

Turning away to hide a grimace, she replayed his words and allowed her eyes to travel to the four white taper candles burning on the mantle. Her neighbors had struggled through their share of tough times over the years, and on days of celebration, they lit a candle for their loved ones.

Seventeen years ago, their young son developed a high fever and later died at the hospital from complications. Eleven years ago, their teenage son died after he was crushed by a bale of hay. When their oldest son married and moved to Lancaster, Pennsylvania, with his new wife's family, the Bylers invited Mariah to spend time with them during the holidays. Her best friend's parents loved and accepted her as one of their own.

"That reminds me—" The words caused Mr. Byler to face her. "You're likely to have company later today. We heard the tree fall in your backyard, and my father plans to get neighbors together to help chop wood."

He glanced out the window into the backyard. "We thank *Gott* the branch fell away from the house."

"*Jah*, that's for sure. This afternoon will be busy, but you won't have to worry about taking time away from the store's big sale this week."

He turned to her and rubbed the back of his neck. The lines in his forehead deepened. "The sale."

Wiping her hands on her apron, Mrs. Byler entered the room with swift steps. Her dark green dress reminded Mariah of the evergreens along the property line between their homes. "Merry Christmas, Child." She gathered Mariah in her arms and planted a gentle kiss on her cheek. "Come, sit. Food is on the table."

Mariah reached into the shopping bag and produced half a dozen muffins. "For you. From my mom. Still warm."

"Delightful. She told me she would send them over. Follow me."

Mr. Byler carried the four white candles into the dining room and placed the holder in the center of the table as they all settled into their seats. "We remember those who can't be with us today, but we celebrate with those who are. Let's say grace." He paused as heads bowed for silent prayers.

Mrs. Byler dabbed the corners of her eyes with her napkin.

"I don't know what we're gonna do when you girls get married." Mr. Byler cleared his throat and took a gulp of water. His pink-rimmed eyes glistened with unshed tears.

"Oh, *Daed*. I'll be around for a while. It's Mariah here you have to worry about." Lydia pointed at her with a thumb.

She faced her friend and raised an eyebrow. "What do you mean by that?"

Lydia chewed a bite of cinnamon roll, a thin line of white icing clung to her lower lip. "You and Josiah. I saw him drop you off at your house yesterday."

Mariah hid her hot cheeks.

"How is Josiah?" Mrs. Byler spread butter on an orange-cranberry muffin. "I ran into his mother at the fabric store. It sounded like they'll have a full house for Christmas."

Though the woman smiled, her lip quivered.

"I guess he's doing okay. We haven't spent much time together lately." A void in her chest caused her to pause. She missed the daily conversations with her dear friend. But she didn't want to string him along while she decided what to do with the rest of her life. He deserved better than that. Didn't she?

"Mariah?" Lydia's voice brought her back to the present.

"I'm sorry. I didn't hear you. What was the question?" She glanced from her best friend to Mr. and Mrs. Byler.

"My *daed* asked about our youth group." Lydia tilted her head and glared.

Understanding her friend's nonverbal cue, Mariah stuck her fork in a strawberry and avoided her friend's stare. "I've enjoyed bowling with the others from our church district.""Amos Schrock came into the store the other day." Mr. Byler rested his fork on his plate and turned to Lydia. "He said you and his daughter have been hanging out with young people from the neighboring district." Though he did not ask a question, his voice rose. A muscle along his jawline twitched.

Lydia pressed her lips in a thin line. "Um—" She took a sip of water. "I've gone out with both groups. I'm trying to find the right fit for me." She kicked Mariah beneath the table.

"I have as well, Mr. Byler." Mariah confessed with confidence because she spoke the truth. "I have spent time in both circles."

"Have you enjoyed yourself?" Mr. Byler crossed his arms and faced Mariah.

Thankful he didn't mention the time she had to ride home

from a party in a police car, she concentrated her thoughts on bowling with Josiah and their other friends. "Yes, sir."

"Glad to hear it." He nodded as if satisfied with her answer. "Another delicious meal, dear." He leaned over and kissed his wife on the cheek. "I best get to splittin' wood. It's not gonna get done unless I get started." Frown lines creased his forehead as he pushed away from the table.

"Girls, give me a minute, and I'll help with the dishes." Mrs. Byler hurried to another room.

With her parents out of earshot, Lydia whispered, "My *daed* found cans of beer hidden in the barn. He never said a word to me about them, but I saw the empties at the bottom of the garbage can when I took the trash to the corner. He's not pleased with me."

"Is that why he asked about youth group? Does he think I'm out drinking with you? He has to know the truth." Mariah struggled to keep her voice low. "I will not lie for you, Lydia."

CHAPTER NINE

The fire crackled, and its warmth soothed her sore back and arms—muscles accustomed to carrying heavy boxes at the hardware store. But all of that conditioning hadn't mattered while working in the Bylers' yard. How many loads of wood had they carried and stacked? She'd lost count. But if not for their close-knit community, it would have taken their neighbors a couple of days to remove the giant oak from the yard. Grateful, she shifted against the couch cushion and groaned. Everyone should be feeling the effects of the afternoon's exertion, yet not one of them complained—except for Mr. Byler.

Seated in the armchair beside her, the man made a similar sound through clenched teeth.

"Would you like another bag of frozen peas for your hand, Samuel?" her mother asked.

"Maybe so." He wiggled his fingers and winced.

"I'll get it." Mariah rose and retrieved the vegetables from the freezer. Returning to the family room, she stepped between Lydia and Mrs. Byler and then weaved around four chairs occupied by her sisters and her mother. Crossing in front of her father and grandmother, seated on the couch, she positioned the bag on her boss's hand with a paper towel between the cold and his bruised and swollen skin. "That branch got you good."

"*Jah*. I fear it's broken. I'll have the chiropractor look at it if it doesn't improve in the next few days."

Mrs. Byler shook a finger. "I don't think so, dear. If you're in as much pain tomorrow, I'm taking you to get an x-ray."

"Guess I don't have much of a choice with this one lookin' out for me."

"Isn't that the truth." Lydia nudged her mother with an elbow. The room fell silent until Mrs. Byler laughed. With Lydia's recent trouble, both families seemed on edge when she cracked a joke.

"We'll warm the pies and set the table." Her oldest sister patted legs of the other two seated on either side of her, and they disappeared down the hall.

"Before we have dessert," Mariah rose from the couch and faced her neighbors. "I wanted to give you each a little something." She gathered a red gift bag and two shirt boxes wrapped in blue printed paper from beneath an end table. The dancing snowmen print still made her smile.

"What cute paper," Lydia said, tearing open the present— the lid fell to the floor, her actions contradicting her words. "Oh, Mariah! I love it." She touched the knit scarf to her cheek. Purple and pink ripples unfolded onto her lap. "And I've needed a new scarf—I seem to have misplaced mine."

Had she checked in Dustin's truck? Or maybe one of the other cars that picked her up late at night? Mariah bit her lip—she shouldn't have these thoughts about her best friend. "I'm glad you like it."

Leaning to her left, she handed the gift bag to Mrs. Byler

and then she passed the second box to her boss.

"Open yours first," he motioned to his wife. "I'll need help with mine."

The tissue paper rustled as she reached in the bag and produced a mason jar of oatmeal raisin cookie mix. She hugged the jar to her chest. "I see you've added butterscotch chips."

"My secret ingredient." Mariah held a finger to her lips as Mrs. Byler rose and crossed the room to her husband.

"I can't wait to bake a batch. Now, Samuel, I'll hold the box and you can tear the paper with your good hand." She loosened a corner.

With minimal assistance, he opened his gift and held the handmade journal, inspecting the fabric cover.

"I know you won't be able to use it until your hand heals," Mariah wrung her fingers. "But I thought you could write your poems and songs and keep them in one place."

Moisture collected in the corners of his eyes. "That's mighty kind of you. I will put it to use, for certain."

Grandma rose from her rocking chair. Creaky floorboards caused the family to direct their attention toward her. "I have a special gift I'd like to give while we're all together." She reached behind a quilt stand and produced a small green bag stuffed with red tissue paper. "For you, Mariah."

"*Mammi*? What's this?"

"Open it." Grandma tapped her toes on the wooden floor.

Mariah smoothed her dress. The bag crinkled when she reached inside and removed a small, thin piece of paper.

"Read it. Out loud."

"Well, it says—Pioneer Trails. Round Trip. Sugarcreek to Pinecraft. And Friday is listed as the departure date."

While her mother clutched her chest, Lydia and Mrs. Byler gasped in unison and her father stood in the corner, wearing a stern expression. Her jaw hung open as her eyes darted from the card to her Grandma's glowing face.

"I'm not sure I understand." Mariah flicked the card between her fingers. "Are you sending me to Florida?"

"I am." Her grandmother's cheeks darkened to a deeper shade of rose.

Mariah scanned the paper a few more times. "How did—?"

"Dessert's ready whenever you are." Her oldest sister entered the family room followed by the other two. "Wait. What happened?"

Lydia jumped to her feet. "Mariah's going to Pinecraft!"

"What? When?" All three sisters crowded around Mariah. One said, "I thought I heard you squeal."

She held the paper up for them to see. "I'm going to Pinecraft!" Her chapped lips stung, but her smile remained.

Her grandmother waved her hands. "Okay, okay. Everyone sit down. I should explain." She stayed silent until the room settled. "Mariah's had her share of troubles in recent months. She needs time to sort through her feelings—to find out who she is. You all have been there. For some, the decision is clearer than for others." Grandma faced Mariah. "I wanted to give you this opportunity."

Her father crossed his arms. "When your *mammi* first proposed this idea to your *mamm* and me, we were opposed. But she had arranged every detail. She made it hard to say no." He and Mr. Byler exchanged a knowing look.

Mariah shook her head. "But what about my job at the hardware store?"

"I said *every* detail." Her father held up his index finger.

Grandma sat forward in her chair. "I've arranged for you to stay with my sister Birdie for a few weeks. She owns a bed and breakfast in Pinecraft, and you will be helping her in the kitchen as well as with household duties."

Her boss removed the thawed peas and placed them on the floor.

"But what about your hand?" Mariah asked. "And the sale? I can't go now. Can the trip be postponed?"

"Don't worry, dear. We'll be fine for a few weeks—it'll be a challenge, but we'll manage, won't we, Lydia?"

Her best friend's face pinched. "You betcha. Of course, I wish I was going with you. You're going to have so much fun!"

Mariah hugged the card to her chest. "*Danke*. This is the best gift."

"We will miss you dearly," her grandmother placed a hand on her shoulder. "But this trip is important for you. The decision to get baptized into the church—or not—is not a decision to be taken lightly."

"Not get baptized?" Father stood and stepped forward. "What are you saying, *Mamm*? This possibility was never discussed."

Mariah held her breath but fought to keep her expression neutral.

"I'm not saying anything, John. I wanted to give Mariah an opportunity I wish someone had given me when I was her age." She faced the sisters. "I didn't tell you girls because I wanted it to be a surprise."

"And it was." Mariah jumped up and hugged the one woman who understood her heart. "*Danke*," she whispered. For years she had dreamed of visiting the Amish snowbird community, to mingle with tourists near the popular destination in sunny Florida.

Her sisters joined Lydia and crowded around her. The volume and frequency of their words told Mariah they were excited for her adventure. She did her best to soak up their suggestions and travel advice.

"Sarasota is gorgeous—white sand beaches, crystal blue water. Oh, you'll have a wonderful time, Mariah."

"Make sure to buy a pint of strawberries at Yoder's."

"Don't forget about Big Olaf's."

"Oh, yeah. They have the best ice cream."

"Okay, wait." Mariah held up her hands. "Let's talk about this over dessert. That's fitting. But I think I need a notebook." She rushed to her bedroom but then sat on the edge of her bed for a minute to collect her thoughts.

She couldn't wait to tell Josiah her big news.

—

Anticipation of a conversation with Josiah trembled through her legs as the buggy bumped down the lane to the Weavers' farm. Fresh powder blanketed the rolling hills rising toward the sky on her right. She and Josiah had sledded down those hills countless times over the years.

Once, when they were ten, she had leaned far to her right, causing the sled to veer off the path and into a thin tree. The sound of breaking bones rang in her ears, and she rubbed her right forearm. Josiah had helped her back to the house and asked for permission to accompany her to the hospital. Had she taken him for granted all these years?

He told her he loved her, yet she hadn't reciprocated the feelings. Now she was excited to tell him about her trip—that she was leaving. How would he take the news?

She followed her family from the buggy into the barn and searched for Josiah among the men wearing wide-brimmed felt hats.

"Merry Christmas." Josiah touched her elbow.

She greeted him with a wide grin. "Merry Christmas. I was looking for you. Did you enjoy your time with family?"

"*Verra* much. Joshua and Anna announced their engagement. They'll get married next month." He glanced across the crowded barn to his older brother and his fiancée who appeared to be spreading their news to others in the community based on the joyful expressions and exchanges of hugs.

"Congratulations to them both. I've always thought early spring would be the perfect time for a wedding." Heat rose to her cheeks. "They make a beautiful couple."

His eyes darted away from the happy pair, and he held her gaze.

Not long ago, hadn't a similar sentiment been said about the two of them? Nervous energy churned in her stomach.

"Is this a good time to talk, or are you needed before worship starts?"

"I have time."

"You're never gonna believe this."

He held out his hands. "What? Tell me."

"My grandma bought me a Pioneer Trails trip to Sarasota as a Christmas gift." She raised up and down on her toes.

"So you're leaving?" His shoulders slumped. "How long'll you be gone?"

"Just a month."

"A month?" The lines across his forehead deepened. "That's four weeks."

She sucked in her lip. Maybe she should have phrased that in a different way. "I know, but I'm sure time will fly."

"For you." He shoved his hands in his coat pockets. "What'll you do down there for a whole month?"

"I'll stay with my aunt. She owns a bed-and-breakfast in Pinecraft, and I'll help her around the house and in the kitchen." The sadness in his eyes proved tough to ignore.

"What about your job at the hardware store?"

"My grandma arranged it all, even got permission for the time off from Mr. Byler."

"When do you go?"

"I leave on Friday."

"*This* Friday?"

She nodded. "And I'll come home three Fridays later."

He lowered his head and inhaled a deep breath, which he loudly exhaled through his nose. "Is this what you really want?"

Voices hushed around them as people found their seats and prepared for the service to begin.

"I thought you'd be excited for me," she whispered.

"You thought wrong." The muscle along his jawline twitched as he turned and walked away.

⸺

After lunch, Mariah found Josiah behind the barn near the fence that separated his family's property from the stretch of land he now owned. His fingers massaged a white tuft of hair between the ears of a brown alpaca.

"There you are. I've been looking all over for you." She lifted her dress and stepped into the snow beside him.

His attention remained on the alpaca, their eyes locked as if they had shared a secret, and their lips were sealed.

"So," she wrung her gloved hands. "I wondered if you'd like to take me home after the singing tonight."

"Not going."

"Not going?"

"That's what I said. Got alotta thinkin' to do."

With an arm wrapped around a fencepost, she reached out to pet a second alpaca that had wandered toward them with a curious look in his eye. "You're a cutie."

"That's Bean. This one's Scooter. They're about a year old now."

Bean nuzzled his face against her arm. When she pulled her hand away, he swung his neck and nudged her for more.

"Looks like he likes you." Josiah turned his attention to the field beyond the farmhouse.

An awkward silence stretched between them. Should she press him with questions that would most likely irritate him even more? Should she go?

She couldn't leave this way—not for a month.

Turning toward her, he shoved his hands in his pockets and then stepped past her.

Grabbing his elbow, she rushed to block his path. "Please, Josiah. Let's not part ways like this."

"Like what? You're the one leaving."

"But not forever."

"You see all this," he gestured toward the farmhouse surrounded by a field dotted with alpacas. "The house, the land, and the animals. This is all mine now. I worked so hard to make this happen—for you. For us. I told you I love you—that I want a future with you—but you don't want the same. I get it now."

"Josiah, I—"

"I'm cold. Gonna head inside. Hope you have a mighty fine time in Florida."

CHAPTER TEN

On the afternoon of her big day, her father steered the buggy into the German Village Center parking lot. She pulled her belongings from the back seat and joined other travelers near the Pioneer Trails bus. Caring less about the long road trip ahead, her mind concentrated on the last conversation with Josiah. He'd worked hard to save enough money to buy the neighbors' farm, and he'd wanted to build a life with her on that land. Why'd he have to tell her that when she hadn't felt the same? And why had he sounded so angry when she told him about Pinecraft? Didn't he understand she wasn't going away forever? She'd be home in a month.

Maybe he was worried she'd get in trouble while away, of course, because she'd given him many reasons not to trust her. But she desired to taste the outside world. She longed for independence, and this was her chance. Why did she feel alone with these feelings?

Her grandmother approached on the sidewalk and smiled. "Why the long face, child?"

"Thinking about Josiah."

The woman patted her arm. "I imagine he'll come around—in time."

"Don't be so sure."

"Well, I'm sure you're going to enjoy your days in Florida." She handed her a shopping bag. "For your trip."

The bus driver slid her suitcase into the storage compartment, and Mariah hugged her family and then climbed in and found her seat. Waving out the window as the bus pulled onto the main road, she scanned the small crowd gathered in the parking lot. If Josiah did love her, why had he not come to say goodbye? She had searched the crowded parking lot for those blue eyes, but he never showed.

Blinking back tears as the bus barreled through the countryside, she leaned her head against her seat. Her eyes flicked from the shadows of rolling hills as they passed by her window to the card she pinched between her fingers. She rubbed her thumb across the words—Round Trip: Sugarcreek to Pinecraft. Nineteen and a half hours to go. Best gift ever.

Uncrossing her ankles, she kicked the insulated cooler near her feet. Grandma had suggested she pack dinner and lunch along with a few snacks since the bus would stop one time in the morning for breakfast. She repositioned against the pillow propped against the window and grabbed the shopping bag Grandma handed her before she boarded the bus.

Since the sun had set in the winter sky, now was as good a time as any to see what her grandmother had packed for her. She fished her hand into the bag, expecting to discover a Sudoku book or a jigsaw puzzle. Instead, her hand hit something soft and fluffy. One pull revealed a lap quilt made from fabric in shades of ocean waters. In the glow cast by her overhead light, her eyes lingered on the coordinating squares of polka dots, stripes, and floral prints.

Smoothing the quilt across her legs, she inspected her Grandma's technique, tracing a finger along the swirls and hearts which had been hand-sewn, with love she was certain, on both sides of the quilt. She fingered a white triangular piece placed over the blue patterned fabric and bent forward to get a closer look.

A fabric envelope?

Beneath the flap, she discovered a piece of paper had been folded and tucked into the small pocket. With quick fingers, she inspected the other pockets.

Seven notes in all. Unfolding the first paper, she promised to read this one and save the others for the days when she missed home—a task that proved difficult the moment her eyes settled on her name penned in her grandmother's perfect cursive curls. Was it her imagination or could she smell cinnamon on this note?

My dearest Mariah,

Knowing you, I imagine it didn't take you long to discover the notes I've hidden in this quilt. I bet you're on the bus headed to Pinecraft, as you read this first letter. With our busy holiday schedules—me helping at the bakery and you working extra hours at Byler's—I didn't get a chance to explain the entire reason I decided to send you on this adventure.

You see, when I was your age, I was being courted by a young Amish man. We had grown up together. My family and those in our community assumed I would marry him, and we would have a large family. But throughout the courtship, I knew I wasn't interested in spending the rest of my life with him. I wanted to work outside the home.

During this time, I worked as a nanny for our English neighbors. The husband traveled quite often, and the wife practiced as a nurse at the local hospital. I enjoyed listening to stories about her patients, and I often dreamed of attending college and becoming a nurse—contrary to the path my parents had laid out for me. They were unwilling to entertain my dreams or to address my doubts about being baptized into the church. Wanting more time to explore the possibility, I asked the bishop for permission to get my GED and enroll in a practical nursing program. He declined my request, and I guess I don't blame him—my betrothed was his nephew. My parents were disappointed with my decision to register in the program despite their objections, especially my mother. My heart still seizes when I think about how I hurt her. I did ask for forgiveness, and I pray she forgave me before she died.

After a year in the program, I decided nursing wasn't in the plans Gott had for my life. I also knew I didn't want to return to my Church District because I didn't want to marry the bishop's nephew. I also feared I would be shunned for going against their wishes and leaving. My older sister had married and moved across the county to live with her husband's family in a neighboring Amish community. I had planned to visit them for an extended time—to help care for her children. I fell in love with the people there, and I stayed.

While there, I often prayed for direction and discernment. One winter, my brother-in-law's family booked a trip to Pinecraft. I was invited to join them to take care of the children. While spending time with his extended family in Florida, I met my brother-in-law's cousin. We enjoyed our time together, and as I prepared to return home, he had asked permission to court me. I got baptized into the church, and we wed the following spring. I was married to your daadi for 40 years before he went to live with the Lord. Best 40 years of my life. Had I not been given time to explore my doubts, my path in life would have led me in a different direction.

While you're away from home, say your prayers and read the Bible. Take advantage of the time you've been given to discover who you are and who Gott wants you to be. I love you dearly, and I look forward to hearing about your adventures.

Blessings,
Mammi

Mariah held the letter to her chest and considered spending the remaining hours on the bus processing this new knowledge about the events in her grandmother's life. Instead, she pulled the quilt up over her shoulders, adjusted her pillow against the cold windowpane, and closed her eyes. For now, she'd rest in peace with the knowledge that someone else understood.

—

Around half past noon on Saturday, the bus pulled into the Tourist Mennonite Church parking lot. As Grandma had promised, a large crowd had gathered to welcome the visitors to Pinecraft. Mariah shielded her eyes from the warm sun as she stepped off the bus. She glanced past the RVs, campers, and golf carts parked in the adjacent gravel lot and peered over the women wearing dresses in shades of turquoise, violet, and magenta. After placing the cooler and shopping bag near her feet, she wiggled her sweaty toes. She couldn't wait to remove her gym shoes and slide into the flip-flops she had packed.

Craning her neck, she looked for her great-aunt—a woman her grandmother claimed bore a strong family resemblance despite her Mennonite apparel.

As the bus driver set her suitcase on the pavement, she spotted a heavyset woman standing behind a group of men wearing straw hats. The lady wore a conservative dress sewn from a light blue patterned fabric, and a white lace coverlet hid her braided bun. She held a brown paper bag in one hand and a leash connected to a black miniature schnauzer in the other. Family and friends greeted one another with hugs as Mariah wheeled her suitcase between the groups.

The puppy barked as she approached. "Aunt Birdie?" she asked.

"Oh, hush, Sunny." The older woman patted the dog on the nose and straightened his bright yellow bandana around his neck. "Mariah. Well, look at you. All grown up." She bent forward and wrapped her in a long embrace. "I haven't seen you since I visited Berlin for Christmas when you were tiny. I'm happy you're here. Of course, I can use a helping hand, but there'll be plenty of opportunity for some relaxation while you're in town."

Mariah smiled. Aunt Birdie's welcome and acceptance warmed her almost as much as the sun's rays.

"How was the ride?" the woman asked.

"There were a few construction zones, and we hit traffic. I was relieved to get out and stretch my legs when we stopped for breakfast."

The puppy crept toward Mariah and sniffed her legs. She reached down and scratched the dog between the ears.

"I'm sure you were. Let's head over to the B&B. We'll get you settled. Maybe later this afternoon we can grab a cone from Big Olaf's." Aunt Birdie touched her forearm. "They have the best ice cream in town."

"So I've heard."

"Afterward we can take a walk, and I'll show you around. Introduce you to some people."

The bus had arrived about fifteen minutes earlier. Now only a few couples remained in the empty parking lot. "Wow. They cleared out quickly."

"Yes. People gather to greet loved ones when they arrive, or they want to grab an issue of *The Budget* fresh from Sugarcreek. They're on vacation. No time to dilly-dally. Come with me. The B&B is a few blocks this way." She looped the leash around her wrist and shifted the brown paper bag in the crook of her elbow. Lifting the bag, she added, "Yoder's, across the street there, has the best strawberries this time of year. Sweet and plump. Perfect for strawberry shortcake."

Mariah skipped along the sidewalk to catch up to her aunt who, unlike her, had not stopped to watch shoppers as they bustled in and out of the market. "The line for the restaurant is wrapped around the back of the restaurant."

"Oh, yes. It's a pretty popular place. In my opinion, their meatloaf dinner is the best, though my friends prefer the fried chicken. And you must get a slice of peanut butter cream pie—or two." Aunt Birdie touched her palm to her belly and chuckled.

"I appreciate the tip." Mariah ran her fingertips over the bridge of her nose and pinched away a memory. Her focus would remain in the present, not the past.

Minutes later, the pair turned the corner and headed away from the main street. Nestled between tidy white cottages stood the grandest house on the block. The spacious front porch extended the length of the light-yellow house and supported flowerboxes for the second story windows. The porch was home to a swing and a pair of rocking chairs painted the color of denim. Remembering the pair of jeans she wore to the field parties brought to mind the painful memories associated with those nights.

She shifted her focus to the bright pink impatiens and orange snapdragons in the beds along the front of the house and touched the delicate petals. "These flowers are gorgeous."

"Why, thank you, dear." Aunt Birdie jostled a key in the deadbolt. "I was hoping you'd help me weed the beds out behind the patio in the backyard in the next day or so. In the spring, I'll plant an additional garden in the space. I'd like to clear it out now so I can prepare the soil. I'm booked solid for the next couple weeks, so I'll also need your help freshening the rooms and preparing meals."

Mariah paused inside the front door. Bright pink flowers from the gardens out front had been snipped and arranged in a delicate glass vase beside a guest book on a table. Several names had been scrawled across the pages. "You just tell me what you need me to do. I'm grateful to you for allowing me to stay here."

Aunt Birdie secured Sunny in his crate and placed the strawberries in a ceramic berry bowl on the kitchen counter. "Let me show you to your room."

Mariah followed her great-aunt into a modest bedroom to the right of the kitchen. The pale pink walls reminded her of the wild mushrooms that grew in late summer throughout the meadows near her home. Memories of Josiah surfaced, and she blinked them away.

"Make yourself at home." The older woman extended her arm toward the bed. "My room's across the hall. I rent the four large upstairs bedrooms to guests. Feel free to look around." Aunt Birdie raised her eyebrows. "Once I finish up my paperwork, we can head out for that ice cream." Leaving the room, she closed the door behind her.

With a grunt, Mariah lifted her suitcase onto the bed blanketed by a chocolate-covered-cherries patterned quilt in shades of pink and cocoa. The luggage lid bumped the headboard, and a beautiful painting of the beach at sunset rattled against the wall. Cringing, she steadied the frame and then removed her blue and white lap quilt from the shopping bag. With a gentle touch, she draped it over the back of a chair in the corner and then slipped her dresses onto hangers and arranged them in the closet. Once she had organized her belongings, she headed upstairs to check out the four guest rooms as Aunt Birdie had suggested.

About an hour after her arrival in Pinecraft, Mariah wandered down the palm-tree lined streets without a care in the world. She and Aunt Birdie stood in line for ice cream behind a small group of English tourists who struggled to decide what to order.

Aunt Birdie stepped closer to Mariah and whispered, "There's really nothing to decide. You must try a scoop of toasted coconut in a waffle cone." She licked her lips.

"Sounds delicious."

The first bite didn't disappoint. The coconut reminded Mariah of Lydia and the Monkey Butter, and she smiled.

"Well, hello." Her aunt waved her hands at a couple of Amish teens. They threw their trash in a nearby garbage can and approached Mariah and her aunt.

"Hi, Ms. Miller." The young woman leaned forward and gave Aunt Birdie a quick hug while the young man stuffed his hands in his pockets and nodded.

"I'd like to introduce you to my great-niece Mariah Mast. She'll be staying with me for a few weeks. Mariah, meet Dixie and Luke Yoder. I'm good friends with their grandmother."

"Oh, Yoder, like the restaurant in town?"

"Yes, but no. Same name. No relation, if you can believe it." Dixie twisted her *kapp* strings. Her peach dress highlighted the warm tones in her skin. "It's a pleasure to meet you. Hey, we're meeting at Pinecraft Park to play volleyball later. Would you like to join us?"

"She would love to." Aunt Birdie smiled with a look of satisfaction.

Mariah shrugged. "Sounds fun."

"I have guests checking in this evening. Would you two mind stopping by the B&B so Mariah can follow you there?"

"You got it." Luke's deep voice surprised her. His eyes were as dark as the smear of hot fudge on his top lip. Resisting the urge to hand him her napkin, she smiled instead. When he returned the expression, butterflies fluttered in her belly.

"You can borrow my bike." Aunt Birdie licked a drip of ice cream as it trickled down the cone, interrupting her thoughts.

"This'll be fun. See you around six o'clock." Dixie turned and headed for the door.

Luke tipped his straw hat and grinned. The butterflies took flight yet again.

Those dimples. No, no, no, Mariah. You came to Pinecraft to find yourself, not a man.

CHAPTER ELEVEN

"Did you sleep well?" Aunt Birdie flipped golden pancakes in a cast iron skillet on the stovetop.

Mariah nodded through a yawn. "The bus ride took a heavier toll on me than I thought. Either that or playing volleyball until it was dark."

"I'm glad you had fun. The Yoders are a wonderful family. Would you do me a favor and prepare a fruit salad?" She pointed the spatula in her hand to the melons and pineapple on the counter. "The guests should be down in about half an hour."

Mariah sliced the cantaloupe in half. "You asked me to weed the flower beds this morning. Is there anything else you'd like me to do today?"

Aunt Birdie poured orange juice into small glasses. "The weeding is the main project for today. Three guests requested dinner this evening, so I'll need your help with food preparation and serving—maybe around 3:30pm?"

"I'll be here. Once I've finished in the garden, would you care if I take your bike for a ride?"

"Sounds like a great plan. Wish I could join you."

"I could ask Dixie to borrow her bike. We could ride to-gether."

"Oh, thank you, dear. But I shouldn't." Aunt Birdie rubbed her right leg. "I don't want this knee to give me any fits, or I'll land back in physical therapy." Her face pinched, and she resembled a pug.

Mariah laughed. "That doesn't sound fun at all."

Later in the morning, she tucked her dress into the waistband of her underwear and knelt in the dirt. The smell of moist earth surrounded her as she rid the garden of weeds one by one.

With a full trash bag beside her, she pushed up from the ground and rounded to the front edge of the garden. A horn honked. She dropped the spade and untucked her dress. Her skirt spilled over her calves, but the top stuck to her waist like another layer of skin. Crossing an arm over the damp fabric, she wiped sweat from her temple as the car slowed near the sidewalk. Luke and two of his friends waved at her through open windows before their driver accelerated, disappearing down the street.

Had he and his friends caught her? Dropping to her knees, she dirtied the dress and silently scolded herself. Her parents turned a blind eye when she and her sisters shortened their dresses while doing yardwork, but this wasn't Holmes County.

Once she'd filled three garbage bags with weeds, she stepped back onto the sidewalk and admired her work. The job had taken longer than expected, but she had time to change her dress and grab a bite to eat for lunch before taking a bike ride through town. In any case, she'd hurry so as not to be late to help Aunt Birdie with dinner.

After gulping down a turkey sandwich and a handful of carrot sticks, she jotted a note for her aunt and headed off to explore. She crossed several streets and passed restaurants and store fronts, closed for the Sabbath. On her way back to the B&B, her forearms began to itch. As she waited for the light to change at an intersection, she inspected the red bubbles that appeared in patches. A man on a scooter pulled up along-side her as an identical tingle erupted on her neck. She couldn't resist the urge to scratch.

"*Gut* day." He tilted his head and inspected her arms with his eyes. "Why, you have poison ivy. You'd best get some ointment on that right quick." He lifted his chin. "There's a dollar store across the street. They carry the cream." The light changed, and he looked both ways before he stepped into the road.

"Poison ivy? Ugh."

⁓

"Try your best not to scratch. You don't want to get an infec-tion." Aunt Birdie mixed baking soda and water in a small bowl. She smeared the paste over the bright red rash that now covered Mariah's arms and neck. "Poor girl. This should help. I hope you didn't get this from my garden."

"I didn't see the vine out there." Mariah paused. "Oh, but I did chase the volleyball into the brush a couple times at the park last night." She sank deeper into her seat on the couch.

A knock sounded on the door. "Who could that be? The guests have keys." Aunt Birdie shuffled out of the kitchen into the foyer.

The front door squeaked as it opened.

"Luke. What a pleasant surprise." Her aunt's voice floated into the kitchen. "Please come in."

Luke?

Her aunt escorted the visitor into the kitchen.

Mariah covered her neck with her hands and forced a smile.

"She's contracted poison ivy." Aunt Birdie patted her shoulder. "And she's not feeling great this evening."

"I heard. That's why I'm here." He set a basket on the kitchen table.

"You heard?" Mariah groaned. "How?"

"My dad said he spoke with you—suggested you go to the store for some ointment. He saw you bike to the B&B and figured you are the girl we hung out with last night. You don't look nearly as bad as he described." Luke winked.

"Gee, thanks." Blood rushed to her cheeks. Maybe he couldn't distinguish blushing from the rash through the globs of paste that made her look like a monster.

"What'd you bring?" Aunt Birdie peeked at the load he had carried.

He removed a purple ceramic pot from the basket. "I was out running errands, and my mother suggested I pick up an aloe vera plant. It should provide some relief."

"How sweet." Aunt Birdie accepted the plant and placed it on the counter near the windowsill.

"I also brought a bunch of bananas." He set the fruit on the table. "And these cucumbers are from our garden. Probably the last for the season."

"Bananas?" Mariah tilted her head.

"My *mammi* said rubbing the banana peel over the bumps can help." He shrugged his shoulders. "As might cool cucumber slices. Maybe?"

"Thank you so much for thinking of me." She giggled, clenching her fists in an attempt not to scratch the nape of her neck.

"Well, I won't keep you ladies."

"You are a thoughtful young man," Aunt Birdie said. "I always knew I liked you."

His cheeks turned pink as he grabbed the basket from the table and backed out of the kitchen.

Aunt Birdie ushered him to the front door after stealing a glance at Mariah.

Mariah opened a banana and pressed the peel to a spot of blisters Aunt Birdie had not yet covered with baking soda paste. Nothing. Wonder how long the peel should stay on her arm? She took a bite of the soft, sweet fruit as her aunt waltzed into the kitchen.

"What a wonderful young man. He went out of his way to bring you these remedies. And he's not hard on the eyes either. Those are the men we ladies want to hold onto." Aunt Birdie rinsed the baking soda paste from the bowl.

Mariah tested the inside of the banana peel on another itchy patch of skin. "He is sweet, but I must remind you I'm not here to get involved with anyone. That's one reason why I needed a break from my life at home."

"Keep an open mind, Mariah Mast. God's timing—while unpredictable—is perfect. I can't wait to see what He has in store for you."

That precise thought stirred in her soul both anticipation and apprehension.

———

Once the dinner dishes had been washed and returned to the cabinets, Mariah retired to her bedroom. She grabbed a book from the shelf in her room and sank across the bed with care not to disturb the quieted itch. After reading the first page of the classic tale, her gaze landed on her Grandma's quilt. Another letter was worth the effort and the chance of discomfort. She slid the note from a fabric envelope and returned to the bed.

My dearest Mariah,

I hope you have settled into the slower pace of life in Pinecraft. The warmth from the sun and the smell of the ocean should be a welcome relief from the cold, gray days at home. Though it's best to face our troubles, sometimes we need a break from routine.

In another letter, I mention my life with your daadi. Atlee was the best husband, friend, father—and daadi—a woman could ever hope for. We were married for 40 years. He was a man after God's heart. When he passed away three years ago, I found myself in the darkest days of my life. A dear friend of mine reminded me of Romans 5: 3-5, "Not only so, but we also glory in our sufferings, because we know that suffering produces perseverance; perseverance, character; and character, hope."

When she shared this scripture with me on that dreary winter morning, I fell to my knees in prayer. I thanked God for the time I had with Atlee. I praised Him for His promises of eternal life in heaven. It wasn't easy, but through this trial, I did find joy in my suffering.

I understand you've been going through some tough times in recent months. My hope is that you'll remember our Lord God loves you. He created you. You are His cherished child. "Trust in the Lord with all your heart. Lean not on your own understanding. In all your ways acknowledge Him. He will make your path straight." Proverbs 3: 5-6.

Embrace this gift of time you've been given.

The poison ivy on her wrist tingled. Find joy in the suffering. Talk about perfect timing. God's voice came through the letter, loud and clear.

CHAPTER TWELVE

Three days later, Mariah started to draft a note to Josiah but then decided against it. Instead, she asked her sisters to pass along her blessings to him in her letter to them. After sealing the envelope, Mariah biked to the Pinecraft Post Office to mail a letter to her family and ship a package for Aunt Birdie. Outside the post office, Mariah paused to peek over the heads of a few children. She scanned the bulletin board for new announcements: garage sale, estate sale, golf cart rental, lost dog, bluegrass band, hymn singing, and Yoder's Construction—Building the Future. Restoring the Past.

Yoder's? She held her index finger to her lips.

"Hey, Mariah." Luke wore a light blue shirt with black pants and matching suspenders.

"I was just thinking about you."

"You were?"

A giggle escaped as she pointed to the bright yellow flyer. "Is this your family's construction company?"

"Yes it is. In fact, I'm on my way to a job site now." He tilted his head toward the post office entrance. "I had to stop in to mail bills to our customers. How are you feeling?"

"So much better." She relaxed her shoulders. "*Danke*, again, for those remedies."

"Which one worked best?"

"Which *one*?" She shrugged. "I used them all."

He laughed. "Glad I ran into you." Facing the bulletin board, he flicked a poster near the bottom. "Would you care to join me—well, us? Dixie and our friends are meeting at this concert and dinner on Friday. The proceeds benefit a camp for youth here in town. We renovated their shelters this summer. Nice place."

She gave the poster a quick once-over, and a sound escaped from her throat. "An Elvis impersonator?"

Luke hung his head and rubbed his neck. "I know, but—"

"No." She touched his arm and lowered her head to look at his face. "I'll be there. Sounds like a lot of fun."

"Great. It's a date." The corners of his mouth curved upward.

"A date?" Her voice squeaked.

He cleared his throat. "An expression. Will you be finished with your work at the B&B at five o'clock on Friday?"

She relaxed her shoulders and nodded. "Check-out is at 11am. I can flip the rooms and have the laundry finished by then. I don't think the new guests are due to arrive until Saturday afternoon."

"How on earth do you finish the laundry in such a short amount of time?"

"My aunt is Mennonite, remember? She uses a washing machine and dryer." Mariah grinned.

"Right. Well, I'll see you Friday."

"See ya." Mariah followed him with her eyes until his straw hat disappeared into the crowds of people along Yoder

Avenue. She turned her attention to the benefit poster. BBQ chicken, baked beans, coleslaw, cookies, and more time with Luke Yoder. No, Mariah. Don't do this.

—

Mariah opened the front door and entered the B&B. Sunny greeted her with a high-pitched bark and a wagging tail.

"Oh, not so fast, mister." She blocked the doorway with her foot.

Aunt Birdie scampered into the foyer. After drying her hands with a dishtowel, she swung it over her shoulder. "Come here, Sunny." She scooped up the dog who proceeded to wiggle in her arms. "The day before you arrived, this little guy had me chasing him all over Pinecraft, didn't you?" She tickled his belly.

When he nibbled on her hand, she placed him on the floor. "Stay out of trouble, or it's back in the crate for you."

"Aww."

"Aww, nothin'. He's a stinker."

Sunny yelped.

"I mailed your box. The postmaster handed me these packages for you."

Aunt Birdie checked the return address label. "I've been waiting for them." She ripped the packing tape and rummaged through the box. "Aren't these cute?" She held up tea towels, each embroidered with different colored flowers.

"For the bathrooms here?"

The older woman shook her head. "A group of ladies are meeting at the Pinecraft Pavilion for a Tea in the Park on Saturday morning. I offered to pick up a gift for a raffle prize."

"Oh, the park. That reminds me. I ran into Luke at the post office."

Aunt Birdie set the towels in the box and perched on the arm of the couch with her hands in her lap. "You did? And..." She widened her eyes.

"Oh, stop." Mariah swatted the air with her hand. "He and his friends invited me to join them for a benefit dinner in Pinecraft Park on Friday evening. Do you care if I go? I mean, once I've flipped the rooms after the guests leave. Is there anything else you need me to do?"

"I don't think there should be a problem. Not on Friday, that is." The older woman rose and crossed the room. After consulting her appointment book, she continued. "I will need your help on Saturday though. I'm scheduled to help set up for the tea early tomorrow morning. Would you mind taking care of breakfast on your own? I think you can handle it."

"You can count on me."

Aunt Birdie stepped close and gave Mariah a quick hug. "It's been wonderful having you here. I'm afraid I won't want to let you go."

"I'm not missing the cold weather back home. And I could get used to these warm days, that's for sure."

"The sunshine is what convinced me to move here from Ohio all those years ago."

The front door clicked. Aunt Birdie crossed the room and entered the foyer. "Have a wonderful day, folks. See you when you return." She waved as the couple stepped off the front porch.

"Mariah, the Johnstons left for the day. Would you please tidy up for them? The peach room—top of the stairs."

"Of course." She grabbed the cleaning supplies from the hall closet and headed up the steps. As she mopped the bathroom floor, her thoughts kept wandering back to Luke. The other night, his rolled-up shirt sleeves revealed tan muscles toned from lifting heavy beams and two-by-fours. She prayed to God, asking if crossing paths with Luke was part of His plan. She wiped the sink dry and promised to stay silent so as not to miss direction.

After folding a load of towels and stacking them in the linen closet, she took advantage of being alone in the house. She grabbed a letter from the lap quilt and a magazine on her way to the front porch. Holding the third note from her grandma, she got comfortable on the porch swing and used her toe to rock back and forth.

My dearest Mariah,

"Hey! What're you up to?" Dixie and two girlfriends stopped on the sidewalk in front of the B&B. Flip-flops peeked from beneath their dresses, all three a different shade of pink.

Mariah rose from the swing. She recognized the Troyer twins from the park. "It's nice to see you again."

"We're on our way to Yoder's for a piece of pie. Would you like to join us?" The tone of Dixie's voice rose.

Mariah could resist the temptation of a tasty treat, but the invitation to spend time with new friends proved too enticing. "I was taking a break. I'd love to join you. Let me grab my purse." She tucked the letter inside the magazine and set it on the porch swing.

—

Leaning toward Dixie, Mariah pressed her forehead against the large picture window at Yoder's that overlooked Bahia Vista Street. Broad shoulders blocked her view of the corner, but from her limited experience, she imagined the line wrapped around the back of the building. "You were right. If we'd arrived any later, we'd be way back there." She gestured with her thumb.

Dixie nudged her with an elbow. "What're you getting? Cherry is today's special."

"Not cherry." Maybe she should order a scoop of ice cream instead. But she didn't want her new friends to ask questions—not when she'd agreed to join them for pie. She reviewed the pie flavors printed on the menu—the same choices written on a wipe-off board near the front door. Both lists overwhelmed her taste buds, but Aunt Birdie's recommendation rang in her ears. "Mmm, I'm gonna go with peanut butter cream."

"Me too." Her friend folded the menu and placed it on the table. "They make the best in town."

"I'll be the judge." Mariah raised an eyebrow. "My family owns a bakery. I have a great deal of experience tasting pies." She bit her lip. Why'd she lie?

"How in the world do you stay so slim?" Dixie's eyes rested on her midsection.

The taller twin leaned forward. "*Jah*, tell us your secrets. Please."

"I don't work there." She laughed.

"Bet that does help. You know, peanut butter cream is Luke's favorite too. But my *daed* loves cherry, so he and the crew are regulars here on Wednesdays." Dixie scanned the restaurant. "Oh, look. There he is now."

Mariah straightened her skirt beneath the table and craned her neck to see around a heavyset waitress who grabbed menus from the stack on the counter and swiveled her hips, leading half a dozen men in the opposite direction.

The bearded man from the street corner sat beside Luke.

"Is the man on the end your *daed*?" Mariah whispered. She touched her neck and grimaced—no need to relive the embarrassing encounter. Maybe he wouldn't recognize her now that the redness from the nasty rash had faded.

The hostess approached their table with a notepad in her hands, and minutes later returned with four slices of pie. Another server stopped beside Luke's table and unloaded lunch platters from her tray.

Mariah dipped the tines of her fork in whipped cream several times before savoring her first bite of the silky, smooth pie. Conversation at the table revolved around the young ladies and their jobs and romantic interests. Mariah remained quiet, listening but with eyes focused on her plate.

"How'd you break your nose?" the shorter twin asked.

Dixie gasped. "Why on earth would you ask her a question like that?"

"What? She has a hump, and I figured she must have broken it at some point."

Warmth rushed to her cheeks and brought with it a memory of Josiah and his devotion. She swallowed hard. "It's okay. I told you my parents own a bakery. I have three older sisters, and growing up, I was always told I couldn't help because I was too little. One day, I tried to prove them wrong. I lifted a full tray of cherry pies from the display case, but it was too heavy." She gestured to show how she'd taken a direct hit. "Broke my nose."

"Ouch." Dixie forked a bite of pie. "How do you feel about cherry pie?"

"Haven't tried it since."

"Is there a guy waiting for you at home?" The taller sister shifted in her seat.

"Me?" Mariah asked.

The girl nodded.

As she cleared her throat, Josiah returned to her mind.

Along with the disappointment she had caused him by leaving. Then she remembered how it felt to dance in Dustin's arms and how he had broken her heart. She wiped her mouth on a napkin. Looking to her right, she caught Luke staring in her direction. A tingling sensation replaced the wave of nausea that accompanied the painful memories.

"Um...no." Mariah shook her head. "Not really. I mean— well, it's complicated." Keeping her hand close to her chest, she waved. Luke placed his napkin on an empty plate and pushed away from the table.

"*Complicated*? Do tell."

Privacy was apparently not a big deal to either of the twins. Mariah waved away the question as Luke approached the table.

Sawdust clung to the waistband of his pants, and Mariah detected the faint scent of lumber when he stepped beside her. He tapped the table. "Funny running into you here."

His sister leaned back in her chair. "We were walking past the B&B and stopped to ask Mariah to join us."

Luke nodded without shifting his gaze from Mariah to Dixie. "Good to see you."

Her heart beat faster. "You'll see me again on Friday night when I tag along to the benefit dinner with you guys."

"Luke told me he invited you," Dixie said. A bright smile stretched across her face. Mariah noted the family resemblance. "Tagging along implies we don't want you there, and that's not the case. I'm glad you want to hang out with us."

"Me too."

"And you must be Mariah Mast." The deep voice startled her.

Luke placed his hand on her shoulder, and she relaxed under his gentle touch. "Mariah, please meet Thomas Yoder, my father." She extended her arm and shook hands with the man whose dark brown eyes sparkled like his son's.

"I see the cream helped clear up the poison ivy." Mr. Yoder stroked his beard.

"The cream *and* all the home remedies Luke delivered— they did the trick." She smiled at the young man who stood an inch or two taller than his father.

"Are you enjoying your time in town?" Mr. Yoder tucked his wallet into his pants pocket.

"Yes. *Verra* much."

A clean-shaven man leaned around Luke. "You ladies remember what happens in Pinecraft stays in Pinecraft. Isn't that right, big guy?" The man slapped Luke on the shoulder. With a cackle, he headed for the parking lot.

Luke blushed and rolled his eyes, then adjusted his straw hat. "On that note..."

"Bye." Dixie's fingers flitted a wave.

"*Jah*, get out of here." The taller twin pushed him from the table. "Mariah doesn't need any more *complications* in her life. Isn't that right?"

Mariah let out a nervous chuckle.

"Now, don't you listen to these boys." Mr. Yoder's eyes reflected a look of concern. "I'm glad to see you've recovered. If you need anything while you're visiting, please let us know."

The hostess dashed past the table and placed the bill in the center of the table.

"Here, I'll divide it up." Dixie reached across her.

Mariah thanked God for the distraction, which spared her

from having to discuss her love life—and the break from it—
with her new friends.

CHAPTER THIRTEEN

On her return walk to the B&B, Mariah paid little attention to the twins' chitchat but instead replayed the conversation with Mr. Yoder and his construction crew. She pictured Luke as he walked into the parking lot. He had looked over his shoulder to find her watching him through the window. His dimple sent her heart racing. No, Luke didn't need to hear about her personal struggles. And she didn't even *want* to discuss those details with the girls, especially not in front of him, that's for sure. What would he think? Would it change the way he looked at her?

She parted ways with her friends, climbing the porch steps two at a time. Spotting the empty swing, she froze. Where was the magazine? She'd left it on the cushion, of that she was certain. Shouldering through the front door, she scrambled through the first floor, overturning throw pillows. A stack of mail on the kitchen island took seconds to rifle through.

Sunny barked. His little paws pattered on the wooden floor leading from the kitchen to the foyer. His yelps then sounded like they were coming from the front yard. The door! Had she forgotten to close it? A lump lodged in her throat as she spotted a streak of black bolting down the street. His bright yellow bandana came to a stop in the grass near the curb.

As she sprinted after the miniature schnauzer, she raised her hands to the sky and sighed a quick prayer. Sunny stopped to sniff around a rose bush in front of a house a few doors down the street. She slowed to a fast walk, hoping not to startle the puppy into resuming the chase.

The dog raised his head and stared in her direction.

"Come here, boy. Want a treat?" Having nothing to offer, she held a clenched fist out to the dog.

Instead of taking the bait, the puppy yelped and took off running through the neighbor's yard. Four blocks later, he stopped again. She bent over and propped her hands on her knees in an attempt to catch her breath.

Sunny barked.

Not again. Hanging her head, she prepared her mind for a longer run.

"Is this your little guy?"

When she heard the familiar deep voice, she lifted her chin and discovered the dog wiggling in Luke's arms.

"Oh, *danke*, Luke. *Danke*." She reached out and wrapped the puppy in her arms. "My aunt would have been *verra* upset had I let him get away." She paused. "What are you doing here?"

He used his thumb to motion across the street. "The work site I mentioned. We're building a garage for the family's golf carts."

She stuck out her lip. "I see."

"I heard someone yelling, and then I saw you running down the street like a crazy person. Thought you could use a hand." He reached over to pet the exhausted puppy.

"A crazy person, huh?" She looked down at Sunny whose tongue shook with his panting. "*Now* you're all worn out. Stinker." She buried her face in the ball of fur. "I better get you home before Aunt Birdie wonders where you are."

Cradling the dog with one arm, she shielded her eyes from the sun with the other.

He brushed his hand against her arm. "If we keep running into each other like this, people are gonna start talking."

His touch, in combination with his smile, weakened her knees. But maybe the trembling was from the run? Yes. Her legs were tired from chasing Sunny all over town. Could he see he'd caused her to blush? She tilted her face toward her shoulder as if to wipe the heat from her cheeks. "See you Friday." She took a few steps backward before she turned away from him.

"The way we're going, we'll see each other before then," he called after her.

One could only hope.

Once she crossed the main street, she remembered her search for the lost letter and quickened her pace. She raced up the steps and shouldered through the door. With Sunny secured in his crate, she resumed her search. The magazine was nowhere to be found—nor were dust bunnies found where they could be expected. Pinching the bridge of her nose distracted her from the disappointment of misplacing her grandma's letter.

Aunt Birdie entered the kitchen through the back door, her arms full of groceries. "Could you give me a hand, dear?"

Mariah flipped once more through a stack of mail on the desk. "Sure. What do you need?"

"I need to whip up a double batch of peanut butter fudge

and could use your help. Would you bring in the last bags for me?"

"Of course." She bent down to look under the kitchen table as if she hadn't checked with thoroughness the first two times.

"Are you okay?"

"I misplaced a magazine. Will you let me know if you see it? The most recent issue of *People*. Princess Kate's on the cover." Mariah ducked out the door.

When she returned to the kitchen with a bag containing sugar, peanut butter, marshmallow spread, and a gallon of milk, Aunt Birdie handed her the magazine.

Mariah dropped the groceries on the table and flipped through the magazine to find the letter still safely tucked between the pages.

"Found it on the porch swing."

"That's where I left it. I'll be more careful next time."

Aunt Birdie smiled. "Oh, and I wanted to ask, did you go for a jog this afternoon?" She placed boxes of rainbow pasta in the pantry.

"A jog?" She drew out the words as she set a package of dog treats in the cabinet.

"Yes. I bumped into a neighbor who told me she saw you running down the street. You may have inspired her to exercise."

"Maybe she'd like to take Sunny for a walk," she muttered.

"What's this about Sunny?" The older woman grinned, and the puppy barked at the sound of his name.

"I'm sorry he escaped, but I caught up to him. He's safe and sound, resting in his crate."

"That's wonderful to hear. Sounds like you've had quite the afternoon. Why don't you enjoy some peace and quiet in your room before the dinner rush? I'll call you when I need your help."

"You don't have to tell me twice." Mariah snatched an apple from a basket on the counter. As she walked down the hall to her bedroom, she held the piece of fruit between her teeth and flipped to the photo collage of the royal family.

In the privacy of her room, she flopped on the bed and unfolded her grandma's letter for the second time that day.

My dearest Mariah,

As you meander your way through life, you will have many great times. I imagine you're enjoying these days spent in Pinecraft. I have fond memories of the times I've spent there. I remember when your aunt and I participated in a shuffleboard tournament at Pinecraft Park. We played well after the sun set, and they had to flip on the lights. One year, your daadi and I played during our visit and won the tournament. The locals congratulated us, but I could see in their eyes, they weren't happy about losing to a pair of snowbirds.

With great times come hardships. I ask you to remember that you will also face numerous struggles in this life. When you feel you can finally keep your head above water, another wave crashes down on you. But Mariah, God prepares us in advance for the challenges that come our way, and He uses these obstacles to mold and form us into the people He created us to be.

Spend time in prayer, my sweet girl. Ask and it shall be given unto you. Seek and ye shall find. Knock and the door shall be opened unto you. It's a blessing we don't have to face

our days alone. At certain times during our lives, God sur-
rounds us with those we need most. We cross paths with people
we would have otherwise never met. I hope you've met some gut
people during your days in Pinecraft. When life gets tough,
lean into your friends, your family, and your community.
Above all else, I ask you to remember to seek the Kingdom of
God first in all you do. When we live our lives to glorify Him,
He will open doors for us, and we are blessed beyond measure.

P.S. Your Aunt Birdie did not get baptized into the Amish
Church. She may be the perfect person with whom to discuss
your doubts about the future.

With love,
Mammi

Mariah read the last few lines through blurry eyes. When she blinked, a solitary tear trickled down her cheek. God had used her grandmother to deliver the message she needed to hear at that specific moment. Though she missed her family and friends, she had never felt this close to God in Holmes County. Did this realization hold any significance for her future?

CHAPTER FOURTEEN

Mariah followed the scent of rosemary to the kitchen.

"Perfect timing, my dear." Aunt Birdie closed the oven door. "I was about to knock on your door. Did you have a nice rest?"

"*Jah*." She touched her chin to her chest and rolled her neck to loosen a kink.

"Could you please mash these potatoes for me?" Her aunt plugged the electric hand mixer into the outlet.

"Do you have a potato masher? I'd prefer to do it by hand."

Aunt Birdie widened her eyes. "I think it's in the drawer by your left hand."

After mashing the potatoes into smaller pieces, Mariah added a stick of butter and poured a cup of heavy cream into the bowl. She used the utensil to force the ingredients to combine. The muscles in her neck and shoulders relaxed. Who knew mashing potatoes was a great way to relieve stress? She seasoned the potatoes with salt and pepper, and then transferred them to a casserole dish.

"Here's a sheet of foil." Aunt Birdie extended her arm. "Please cover the dish and place it on the table. We'll have eight guests for dinner tonight."

"This will be the largest crowd you've had in the dining room since I've been here." She did as instructed and straightened a wayward fork on a napkin before returning to the kitchen.

"You're right." Her aunt jotted a note on a pad near the telephone and straightened a newspaper on the counter. "The weather forecast for tomorrow is beautiful. People will head out to the beach. You should check it out."

"Maybe. Don't you have work for me to do? I don't want to take advantage. And tomorrow's Thursday. My friends are scheduled to work." Voices echoed in the dining room, and she turned to greet the guests.

Serving others at her aunt's B&B fulfilled her in ways she hadn't experienced in her years at the hardware store. As she passed the rosemary chicken and mashed potatoes around the table for seconds, she smiled at the red-haired woman in the seat across from her.

The woman put a finger to her lip before scooping a dollop of mashed potatoes onto her plate. "Would you happen to have any beach towels we could borrow tomorrow?"

"Yes. I can grab them from the linen closet after dinner." Aunt Birdie refilled glasses of water. "I was telling my niece here that she should spend some time on the beach. She's not been there yet."

The woman consulted her three girlfriends with a quick glance. "Well, why not ride there with us?"

"That's a lovely idea." The lady at the end of the table looked like a tourist in her green dress dotted with small white palm trees; her bleach blond hair swept up in a ponytail.

"So it's settled." Aunt Birdie clapped her hands and held them at her chest.

"W-what? Wait—" Mariah raised her eyebrows.

Aunt Birdie patted her back. "After dinner, run over to the Yoders' and borrow a swimsuit from Dixie."

She gasped. "I'm not borrowing a swimsuit."

The woman in the palm tree dress studied her from head to toe, forcing Mariah to step behind a chair. "I have a suit that should fit you." She lowered her voice. "Don't worry. It's modest—and brand new. I picked up a couple for the trip."

"Are you talking about the little black number?" asked the red-haired woman.

The woman nodded.

"Perfect."

"Right? We can trade—towels for a swimsuit."

Mariah smoothed her dress against her legs. "Oh, I don't know."

As the friends nodded in agreement, Aunt Birdie leaned close and whispered, "You're on vacation."

Mariah sighed and cleared dirty dishes from the table. "I'll grab the towels."

—

Standing in the center of her bedroom, Mariah stared at her reflection in the mirror. She turned and twisted to view her exposed body at different angles. Though the borrowed swimsuit could not have hugged her curves any better, she hadn't decided whether or not to wear it in public. She slid her hands over the slick black fabric along her ribs and rested her palms on her hips. It was odd to have a mirror in her bedroom because she had been taught it was wrong to admire her body. Guilt and shame struggled to replace confidence and pride while her eyes lingered on her reflection a few moments longer.

As she slipped into her pajamas, she couldn't resist wondering what Luke would think of her new look. And what about Josiah? Josiah. She hadn't given their relationship much thought since she'd been away, but the pangs of guilt grew sharper when her thoughts wandered to Luke and the special friendship developing between them. She tossed the suit into the bag that held sunscreen, lip balm, a towel, and a romance novel.

Excited for a new adventure, she slid under the sheets and forced her mind to drift toward dreams: Luke's arms around her waist as they swayed to the music performed on stage by an Elvis impersonator at the benefit dinner. Luke walking her home under a starlit sky, his strong hand warm against her palm. As her eyelids grew heavy, she prayed God would give her a sign. Could He please lead her in the direction she should go?

The hallway floorboards creaked, and she opened her eyes. Sunlight streamed through the curtains. The large red numbers on the alarm clock indicated she had overslept—again. She hurried to get dressed, pulling a purple dress over the cute swimsuit. Grabbing the bag, she headed into the kitchen to help with breakfast.

"Good morning, sleepyhead. I set these granola bars and apples out for you to take with you today." Her aunt reached into the refrigerator. "And here are a couple bottles of water."

"*Danke*, Aunt Birdie. It's *verra* generous of the guests to give me a ride to the beach, but I'm having second thoughts. I won't know anyone there."

"But you'll be surrounded by people. Take a book. Spread

out a towel and relax. You'll love the white sand. And the water is bluer than any blue imaginable." Aunt Birdie arranged bagels on a platter.

"I've seen pictures of Florida beaches in magazines we sell at the hardware store, but I'm sure they're more beautiful in person."

The four girlfriends filed into the dining room, leaving their bags and towels in a pile on the foyer floor. Mariah glanced from their bright cover-ups to her plain dress. Was she making the right decision? Or would this be another big mistake?

The lady with bleached blond hair spooned fruit into her bowl. "How does the suit fit?"

"Oh, it's like it was made for me." She fought a smile.

"We're glad to give you a ride to Siesta Key, but last night, we made dinner plans in St. Armands Circle. We won't be coming back here until later in the evening. I wish I had known so I could have mentioned this earlier."

Aunt Birdie placed a tub of cream cheese on the table. "She could jump on the SCAT when she's ready to return."

The red-haired woman pointed toward the foyer with a butter knife. "I saw a list of bus routes and times on a brochure near the front door."

Mariah pressed her lips together. "You know, I'm gonna stay here after all. Please know I do appreciate the invitation."

"Are you sure, dear?" Aunt Birdie touched her shoulder. "You've been looking forward to it. I could arrange for a driver—"

"It's okay. Really. I'll have plenty of opportunities to enjoy the beach. And I can invite Dixie to join me. I would prefer to stay here today." Her cheeks burned under the stare of those seated around the table.

"Well, we're leaving at nine. I feel awful about this. Please let us know if you change your mind." The woman with bleached blond hair buttered a crisp piece of toast.

"I'll wash your swimsuit today and leave it on your bed. I appreciate your generosity." Mariah refreshed the woman's cup with coffee from a carafe.

"That'll be fine." She set the bread on the table.

"I hope you ladies enjoy your day. Excuse me." Mariah swiveled her hips as she moved through the dining room toward the kitchen. Once hidden from view, she ran her hands along her ribs one last time and felt the swimsuit slick against her skin.

CHAPTER FIFTEEN

Mariah dressed the mattress in the light blue guest room with a fresh set of sheets. She covered the bed with a quilt straight from the dryer, admiring the red, white, and blue sawtooth star pattern as she pressed the wrinkles flat with her palm.

Though she had already flipped the green room, tossed in a load of laundry, and baked a batch of cookies, this day could not go fast enough. Luke would arrive around five o'clock to pick her up for the benefit dinner. She hurried to finish the rest of her work, allowing plenty of time to get ready for their date.

No. This was not a date. But the reminder did not stop her from whistling as she scrubbed the powder room floor.

She rushed through a shower and pulled on a fuchsia dress—the one Josiah told her brought out the green in her eyes. With her hair in a braid, the grandfather clock in the living room struck the fifth note, and a knock sounded on the front door. She hurried through the kitchen to answer, adjusting her *kapp* along the way.

"Luke." She couldn't help but greet him with a smile.

He wore a crisp white shirt, navy pants and suspenders, and a straw hat. Without speaking a word, he stood at the threshold and stared.

"Is there jelly on my face?" She covered her mouth with one hand and spoke through her fingers. "I snuck a thumb-print cookie right before you arrived."

"You look mighty pretty in pink." He stepped close—very close—and then tilted his head.

Not until that moment did she long for their first kiss. She lowered her hand and closed her eyes.

"Wait, open your eyes. I wanted to get a better look." He paused. "I hadn't noticed the color of your eyes. Maybe it's the pink dress or the time of day—"

"Oh, right." The blunder caused warmth to rush up her neck and into her cheeks. She turned away from him. "I, uh—I should tell my aunt I'm leaving."

"I'll wait here." He stepped back and leaned against the porch railing. "The others will meet us at the park. Since I was coming from the job site, I offered to swing by to pick you up."

She nodded and rushed behind the door. Taking a deep breath, she exhaled slowly to regain her composure. After calling a goodbye to Aunt Birdie, she grabbed her bag and met Luke on the front porch.

"Ready?" He covered his sandy blond hair with his straw hat. "I thought we could walk. The park's not far. Is that okay with you? I mean, we could run, if you'd prefer." He nudged her with his elbow.

"You think you're so funny." She edged her shoulder into his side. The smell of lumber on his clothes no longer lingered. Instead, she detected the faint scent of ginger root.

As they walked along the sidewalk, Luke told her about an

English client for whom they were building a garage. Engrossed in his descriptions of the woman's house, she stepped off the curb into the path of oncoming traffic. He reached out and grabbed her hand, stopping her from getting hit by a minivan.

"Watch yourself." He pulled her body against his.

While wrapped in his strong arms, she relaxed into the embrace, surprised by how much she enjoyed his touch. Much better in real life than in her dreams.

"*Danke*," she said, her voice a breathless whisper. Could he hear the thump of her heart? The rapid rhythm pumped loudly in her ears. His lips were so close she could smell his mint chewing gum, and she parted her lips.

A car pulled to a stop beside them. The driver honked the horn and motioned for the pair to cross the road.

Luke blinked and released his hold on her. Clearing his throat, he said, "Guess we can cross safely now."

Allowing her breath to escape, she fell into step beside him. Had the car not interrupted the moment, would he have kissed her? Or was it wishful thinking? Josiah had kissed her—once when they were about eleven—during a game of Truth or Dare. Kissing Luke would have felt much different, of this she was certain.

They walked in silence as they followed a path, which ran alongside the creek, and stepped aside to allow bikers to pass.

"If you're hungry, we should get in line for dinner." He pointed to a group of older adults as they filed behind one another near the shelter. "It's still early, but there's already a large crowd here."

She nodded and led him to the back of the line. "By the time we get our food, I'll be ready to eat."

Luke fished around in his pocket and removed a few bills.

Mariah spotted Dixie headed in their direction and waved.

"Hey. So glad you could join us." His sister said as they exchanged a quick hug. "You remember the Troyers." She extended her arm toward the twins dressed in shades of purple and then gestured to a third girl with dark hair and pink lips. "I don't think you've met Sarah yet. Mariah, Sarah." Dixie used her hands to make the introductions. "Sarah. Mariah."

"Nice to meet you." The girl's light-yellow dress swirled around her legs as she hurried to stand between Mariah and Luke. "Hi, Luke." Pressing her shoulder close to him, she touched his hand.

Mariah studied Luke's face. He mumbled a hello as he shuffled the money in his hands.

Sarah shifted her focus to Mariah. Her blue eyes sparkled like the ocean in the sun. "Dixie tells me you're in town for a few more weeks. We work together in the gift shop at Yoder's. How do you like Pinecraft?"

"I'm having a fun time, for sure. Luke and Dixie have made me feel welcome by inviting me to hang out."

"Luke was telling me *all* about the past few days."

"He was?" Mariah glanced at Luke who was conversing with the clean-shaven guy who worked on Mr. Yoder's crew.

"He tells me *everything*." Sarah flicked her wrist.

Everything? She stared at the back of Luke's head. What had he told Sarah about her?

Was there anything to tell? Perhaps she had misunderstood their connection?

"...*Rumspringa*?"

She returned her attention to the girl with pink lips. "I didn't hear your question."

"I asked if you're enjoying your *Rumspringa*?"

Mariah nodded. "I turned 18 in the fall. I prefer the sing-ings over the parties. How about you?"

Sarah looked over her shoulder. "Luke has taken me home from a few singings." She raised her eyebrows. "I'm hoping he asks to court me soon."

The news knocked the wind out of her.

"Isn't it exciting?" Sarah touched her arm.

"Oh, *jah*. I'm happy for you—both."

The girl took a step backward. "Did I say something wrong?"

"Um, no. Please forgive me. Hearing of your relationship reminded me why I came to Pinecraft." Memories of Dustin and Josiah and the heartbreak that followed flooded her mind.

"What do you mean?" Sarah asked.

"It's complicated." The taller twin grinned. Moving for-ward, Mariah would watch what she said in front of that girl.

Luke faced them. "We're next. Where'd Dixie go?"

"The others went to find seats. I told them we'd grab din-ners for them." Sarah placed her palm in the small of Luke's back.

Mariah turned away, pretending to scan the picnic tables for their friends.

"There they are." Luke pointed across the shelter before taking two plates of food from the volunteer. "Follow me."

As soon as they reached the table, another group of teens sat down.

"Go ahead and sit together," he instructed the girls as he set a plate in front of his sister. "Mariah and I can sit over here." Luke lifted his elbow toward a neighboring table.

Though she could feel the weight of a stare upon her, Ma-riah refused to make eye contact with Sarah. Luke nudged her with his elbow. "Is this seat okay with you?"

Luke handed Mariah a napkin, which drifted to the ground on a gentle breeze. She leaned down to pick it up and glanced at the table of girls. Her new acquaintance glared at her through squinted eyes.

"Sarah looks unhappy. Do you think it's because she's not sitting near you?"

Luke didn't turn but shrugged. "Probably so. But you know—"

Mariah gave him time to complete his thought, but he remained silent.

"No, I don't know." She swallowed a bite of baked beans.

Luke scanned the picnic shelter and then made direct eye contact with her. "I'm 19 years old. I enjoy my job in construction. I have great friends. Faith is important to me, but—" He cut into his piece of barbecued chicken.

"But what?" Mariah held her breath, unsure of the direction of this conversation.

Luke leaned on his elbows and lowered his voice. "Please don't think poorly of me, but I'm not sure I want to be baptized in the church." He scooped a spoonful of coleslaw into his mouth.

Mariah reached across the table and grabbed his hand. Since her actions were being observed from the other table, she released her grip and picked up the fork.

"I don't know why I shared this with you. But it's not what you're thinking."

"Luke, regardless of the situation, I'm relieved to hear someone else say this."

He glanced up from his plate. "You are?"

She nodded and poked at her chicken with her plastic knife. "I've been wrestling with my thoughts too. I'm glad

I'm not alone in my struggles. That's why I'm here in Pine-craft—to take a break from all the pressure at home, I guess."

"Well, aren't you too looking cozy?" Sarah appeared behind Luke. She rested her hands on his shoulders.

His eyes lifted to meet hers. "How's your dinner?"

"Lonely."

He winced. "I'll be finished eating in a couple minutes. Maybe we can all head over to listen to the concert. We'll meet you by the shuffleboard courts. Okay?"

"I'm looking forward to it." Sarah's focus remained locked on Mariah as she returned to her seat.

"See you soon." He broke his cookie in half. When she was out of earshot, he continued. "I'd like to continue this conversation when we won't be interrupted. Would you want to go to the beach with me on Sunday? I don't have plans, and I'm interested to hear what you have to say."

"I'd love to, Luke. But what about Sarah?"

"What about Sarah? We've been friends since we were little."

She picked at her chicken. "Sounds to me like you're more than friends."

"My family's in construction, and her family owns the lumber mill in town. Our families would love for us to be husband and wife. Perfect, right? But I don't see a future with her."

"I see how that might pose a problem for you."

He glanced over his shoulder as Sarah stomped away. "I'm not sure you do."

—

"It's late, and it's dark." Luke faced their friends. "Why don't you girls head home together, and I'll walk Mariah to the

B&B."

"Oh, you don't have—"

He held out his hand as if to tell her to stop. "I will see you get home safely."

"*Danke.*" She studied her feet to avoid Sarah's icy stare.

"Sounds *gut*. Glad you could join us, Mariah." Dixie gave her a quick hug. "This was fun. We'll see you soon." She linked arms with two friends, and they bumped into each other as they walked down the sidewalk.

Sarah stepped beside him. "Will I see you tomorrow?"

"I've got to help my *daed*, but I'm sure we'll see each other at church on Sunday. Have a *gut* night." He tipped his hat and looked at her from beneath the brim.

Her shoulders dropped, and then she huffed and hurried to catch up with the other girls.

Mariah lifted her eyes and met Luke's gaze.

He held his breath in his cheeks and blew it out between his teeth. "Most of the time she's a sweet girl—relentless, but sweet."

"Can't blame her." The words escaped and rang in her ears before her brain registered she had spoken them out loud. Her face burned, and she was grateful for the darkness as she scrambled for something to say. "What time would you like to head to the beach on Sunday?"

"Are you going to church?"

"It depends on the amount of work Aunt Birdie needs me to do. Could we plan to meet up around lunchtime, just in case I can't make it to the service?"

"Sure. The SCAT doesn't run regular routes on Sundays, so it'll take us a lot longer to get to Siesta Key. I'll ask my dad's driver if he could run us out there. He or his son may offer to bring us back home. Otherwise, we'll have plenty of time to talk."

"I'm already looking forward to it."

"Me too." A smile stretched across his face and he shoved his fists in his pockets. "Well, you ready?"

Silence lingered between them as he escorted her to her aunt's house. For her, the silence felt comfortable. As the B&B came into view, she wished their night didn't have to end. She could invite him to sit with her on the porch swing? But it was already late, and she had to get up early.

He waited for her to open the front door with her key and took a couple of steps away from her when a guest passed by the window. "I had fun tonight."

"So did I."

"How 'bout this. If I don't see you at church, I'll stop by afterward, and we can grab lunch on our way to the beach."

"I'll be ready." She closed the door, locking it behind her, and then stood by the window until his silhouette disappeared into the darkness.

Through the golden glow cast by a lamp on the table in the foyer, she tip-toed to her bedroom and slid into her pajamas without a sound. With her evening routine complete, she stretched out on her bed and read four chapters in the new romance. Between the description of a first kiss between the hero and heroine and the anticipation of a day at the beach with Luke, she stared at the ceiling through wide eyes.

CHAPTER SIXTEEN

The alarm rang earlier than Mariah expected. Last she remembered, the clock on her nightstand glowed 3:30 a.m., and she regretted the late night. She untangled her legs from her covers and stretched her arms. Rubbing her eyes, she sat up with a groan and rested her feet on the floor. She splashed her face with cold water and then shuffled into the kitchen.

Aunt Birdie had kept simple plans for this morning's breakfast. Since all beds in the B&B were occupied, Mariah was grateful for an easy menu. Since her eyelids still felt heavy, the overhead light in the kitchen remained off. She retrieved parfait glasses from the cabinet and then grabbed yogurt and a container of assorted berries from the refrigerator.

She yawned and stretched again as sunlight peeked through the windows. Reaching into the pantry, she pulled a package of graham crackers off the shelf. With a sleeve of graham crackers in a plastic baggie, she crushed them into small pieces with a rolling pin. They'd serve as a delicious topping for the parfaits.

An hour after she'd risen, platters of golden muffins,

bowls of fruit, and the parfaits, worthy of being featured in a magazine, covered the long table Aunt Birdie had Mr. Yoder fashion from reclaimed wood. Mariah greeted each of the twelve guests as they arrived in the dining room and provided water, juice, and coffee as requested.

While in the kitchen searching for an assortment of tea for an older woman, coughs and groans sounded from the other room. She dropped the box of tea bags and raced to the guests.

"Is everything okay?"

"What is in this parfait?" The older woman's husband covered his pursed lips with a wrinkled hand.

"Yogurt, berries, and graham cracker crumbs." Mariah counted the ingredients on her fingers as she spoke, then bit her lip. So easy. What possibly could have gone wrong? She hadn't thought to check the expiration date on the yogurt container, but it was brand new.

A young lady seated across the table bent forward and sniffed the parfait glass. She crinkled her nose and raised her napkin to her mouth. "I don't think so. You may wish to check again."

Mariah rushed into the kitchen and ripped the graham cracker box from the counter.

Canine Cuisine Dog Treats? What? On no! How?

The older couple wandered into the kitchen.

Clutching the box to her chest, she spun to face her aunt's patrons with tears in her eyes. "I'm so, *so* sorry." She blinked, allowing the tears to spill down her cheeks. "I made a terrible mistake. I didn't sleep well last night, and I'm tired this morning, and I—I switched the packages."

The man extended his hand.

She placed the box of dog treats in his palm. Unable to bear his disapproval, she hung her head. "Please forgive me."

"Dog treats?"

Muffled giggles and loud cackles erupted around her. The man stepped forward and touched her arm. "Don't cry, honey. It was an honest mistake." He nodded toward his wife who was doubled over, her face beet red, matching the roses printed on her dress. "You should hear the stories I have about this one. Do you have more yogurt and berries? Maybe you could serve us each another dish—without the dog treats this time." His wide smile caused the wrinkles around his eyes to deepen.

Mariah wiped her tears with a dishtowel. "I can't believe I did this. *Danke*—thank you for extending grace." There would never come a day when she'd be able to laugh about it.

The woman stepped further into the kitchen. "I'll help you dish them up. May I?" She reached for the refrigerator door.

Another guest, wearing a Siesta Key t-shirt and shorts decorated with tropical fruits, patted her arm. "This will be our little secret," he whispered as everyone settled back into their seats around the table.

"Is there anything else I can get for anyone?" She used a towel to catch a drop of coffee as it trickled down the side of the carafe. The clinking of spoons against glass allowed her to relax her shoulders.

"Now *this* is delicious." The older man nodded. "Great job, young lady."

First Sunny. Then Sarah. Now this. Mariah retreated to the kitchen and praised God for surrounding her with this supportive and understanding group of people. She had escaped certain disaster once again.

A short time later, she stood at the kitchen sink, washing and drying dishes. The dining room table had been reset for the next meal, and both sets of parfait glasses were returned to the cabinet. Aunt Birdie never had to know.

Needing to rest, Mariah flopped face-first onto her bed. A corner of the pocket quilt caught her attention from beneath the bed. It must have slid off the chair in her rush to get ready for the day.

She pulled back the fourth envelope flap and wiggled the note from the pocket. After draping the quilt on the chair, she rolled onto her back and rested her head on the fluffy pillow.

My dearest Mariah,

While we are on this earth, we must pour ourselves out for others. In doing so, we may make mistakes. I encourage you to make mistakes—make them early and often. When we make mistakes, God uses those experiences to shape and mold us. We learn from our errors and grow, coming closer to who God created us to be.

During the short time I studied to be a nurse, I shadowed my instructor during her rounds. It was my first time on the floor. She gave a patient an injection in his shoulder. When she withdrew the needle, blood spurted from his arm and splattered on the wall. I fainted. I then realized God had not planned for me to be a nurse. Entering the program was my mistake, but it's funny, I wasn't even the one who made the mistake that caused me to leave. Had I not fainted at the sight of blood, I may have remained enrolled. But because I left the program, I moved to live with my sister and her family and later met your daadi.

Own up to your mistakes. Take responsibility for your actions as well as your inactions. Apologize when necessary, and ask for forgiveness from those you hurt as well as from the Lord.

Proverbs 16:3 says, "Commit to the Lord whatever you do, and He will establish your plans." When you empty your cup, others may be filled. While it's not our job to fill the cups for others, it's our job to empty ourselves and trust God will meet the needs of others. I will close with one more scripture: Matthew 5:16 "Let your light so shine before men, that they may see your good works and glorify your Father in heaven." I can't wait to hear all about this adventure.

With love and blessings,
Mammi

Two lines jumped off the page, and she reread them three times.

Own up to your mistakes. Take responsibility for your actions as well as your inactions. Apologize when necessary, and ask for forgiveness from those you hurt as well as from the Lord.

It was an honest mistake...It's our little secret...Aunt Birdie never had to know.

Mariah placed the note next to her on the bed. In her mind, the area of gray between black and white widened. Shifting onto her side, she gazed out the open window. A gentle breeze blew through the magnolia tree in the side yard, filling the room with a creamy sweet scent.

The front door slammed, interrupting her thoughts.

She rose and rushed to the foyer. "Hi, Aunt Birdie. How was the tea?"

"Delightful. And the raffle generated more money than we had anticipated." Her aunt walked into the kitchen and placed her purse on the kitchen island. "How'd breakfast go?"

"About that." Mariah wrung her fingers. *Own up to your mistakes. Take responsibility for your actions.*

"What happened?"

"You might want to sit down for this."

Her pleasant expression hardened. "I'll stand."

"O-okay. Well, I accidentally switched the graham crackers."

"With?" Her aunt stretched the word into two syllables.

Mariah bit the inside of her lip. "Dog treats."

"Dog treats!" The woman's face turned so red it looked purple. "Mariah Mast! I gave you one—"

"Please. Wait." She raised her hands in surrender. "It's okay."

"It's certainly not okay. This bed-and-breakfast is my livelihood, and I do everything in my power to keep my guests coming back. And those guests write reviews. I depend on those reviews—*good* reviews—to draw new guests here. Serving dog treats for breakfast? That could ruin me."

"I understand. I meant that once the mistake was discovered, the guests helped me dish up more parfaits. They even joked with me and told me they wouldn't speak of it. I'm terribly sorry for disappointing you. I hope you can forgive me."

"Of course I forgive you." Aunt Birdie wrapped an arm around her. "And now that you've told me the entire story, it seems I may have overreacted. Nobody got hurt. No one has called me to complain—yet. Believe me, they would."

"It won't happen again. I promise."

"Good. Now, put on an apron. I need you to help me with the baking."

CHAPTER SEVENTEEN

On Sunday afternoon, Luke's driver pulled the car to a stop near the sidewalk, and Mariah climbed into the back seat.

The man's phone beeped. "That's unfortunate." He studied the screen. "Due to construction on Bahia Vista, I was going to drive down through Bee Ridge. But there's a wreck—three cars—and my app's telling me the fastest route is to go north and west to get to 41. Looks like it'll add 15 min to the drive."

Luke shifted in his seat and smiled at Mariah. "Good with me." His celery-colored shirt brought out the golden flecks in his brown eyes.

"Me too."

"It's settled then." The driver checked over his left shoulder and then pulled away from the curb. "You two excited? Got a great day to go to the beach. Clear and sunny, not too hot."

"Mariah's never been to the beach. Can you believe it, Mack?" Luke faced forward.

"No?" The man's bushy eyebrows raised above his thick-rimmed glasses. "Where you from?"

"Ohio." She clutched the bag she'd packed with a beach towel and a bottle of sunscreen against her hip and then leaned against the back seat into the warmth shining in through the rear window. "My sisters wrote to tell me they're expecting snow this week." She shivered at the thought. "When I go home, I'll miss the weather here, for sure."

While the conversation between Luke and Mack centered around baseball, she craned her neck to see the tops of the Sarasota high-rises out her window. They rounded a bend, and the glass-front hotels reflected shades of blue she'd never seen before. Puffy white clouds appeared on the horizon.

"This your first time to Sarasota?" The driver spoke to Mariah through the rearview mirror.

"*Jah.*" A marina appeared on her right as they came to a stop at a red light. Fishing boats, white sailboats, and docked yachts held her attention until the car accelerated, and they passed out of sight. "I love it here."

"Keep your eyes peeled." The man ducked below the sun visor and pointed. "Right up here, we're gonna pass the city's most visited spot—this statue. Here." He slowed to a stop at another red light.

She unbuckled her seat belt and slid behind Luke. The statue rose into the sky two, maybe even three stories. A sailor embraced a nurse—her back arched, her lips locked with his. A couple posed in a similar position beneath the nurse's skirt while a third person captured the moment on camera. "Wow. I—"

"So," Mack turned to Luke as the car rolled through the intersection. "What d'ya think of those Braves? Got a chance this year?"

Resting her head against the window, Mariah clung to the

vision of the nurse in the arms of the sailor. She remembered her grandmother's story about wanting to become a nurse followed by the note about the love her grandparents shared for each other. What might it feel like to recreate that scene with the guy riding in the passenger seat? As water replaced the land around her, she allowed her mind to wander.

"Alrighty." Luke's voice floated into the back seat. "We made it."

Mack steered the car into a parking spot adjacent to a bike shop. Mariah gathered her belongings, and Luke met her near the front of the car.

"Pick you up here at what, five?" The man slapped the driver's side door.

"We'll be here." Luke gestured for her to walk in front of him, past a row of bicycles arranged in a line against a wall to their left. They rounded the building, and he held the door open for her.

The store owner had the two of them sign waivers and complete a rental agreement before providing a map of town. Mariah followed the petite woman's finger—her nails painted a bright shade of coral—as she traced a bike route to Siesta Beach.

"This way you stay off the main roads." Her voice sounded hoarse. "You can ride on the sand, but remember to walk your bikes when you're in between the life guard stands on the public beach. You are welcome to choose any of the bikes out there against the yellow wall." After she folded the map and handed it to Luke, she glanced at the large-faced watch on her wrist. "And be back by five."

"We'll be back before then." Luke folded the receipt and slipped it in his bag.

Once outside, he mounted a dark purple bike with thick

tires while Mariah selected a bright yellow bike with a basket big enough for both of their bags. They pedaled down sidewalks until the traffic cleared and then crossed into a bike lane on the main road. As she pumped the pedals, the briny air filled her lungs. Though trying her best to pay attention to the cars speeding past her, she swung her head from right to left so as not to miss a cute store in which she might find a souvenir.

Within ten minutes, the sugary white sands of Siesta Beach squished between her toes. Red rental umbrellas shaded families from what would soon be the heat of the day. Tan bodies splashed in the clear, cobalt blue water as it rose in frothy waves before breaking on the beach. A small child wearing a diaper toppled over when a strong wave hit him. His mother pulled him to his feet and rescued his bucket and shovel from the surf. Mariah giggled.

They secured their bikes on a rack, scoped out a location, and spread their towels. She pulled her dress up over her calves and straightened her legs across the pink and orange stripes, allowing her feet to sink into the sand.

"I brought lunch. Hungry?" A wrapper wrinkled as Luke pulled two packages from his bag. "One's turkey and mustard. The other's turkey and mayo. Both with the works."

"The works?"

"You know, cheese, lettuce, tomato, and a slice of pickle."

Mariah selected the sandwich with mayonnaise and accepted a small bag of chips. She slid the dill spear from the wrapper and took three bites of the flesh, placing the rind on a napkin beside her.

"Hope you like root beer." He handed her a bottle of soda. "It's all we had in the fridge."

"Love it."

"Interesting."

"What? That I like root beer?"

"No." He pointed at the half-eaten pickle. "The way you eat a spear."

"I only like the part with the seeds."

"Really? Can I finish it?"

"I guess." She tugged a corner of the napkin closer to him.

"The rind's the best part," he said around a bite.

"Gross. Didn't your mother ever tell you not to talk with your mouth full?" She nudged him with her elbow.

Luke fell onto an extended elbow.

A gentle breeze blew and a small stack of napkins near his feet fluttered into the sand.

He scrambled to collect them and shoved them into his bag. "Clean beaches are important to me. Sometimes after big storms, I'll come out with other volunteers and pick up trash. I've found everything from pieces of boardwalks, to soda cans, to turtle nest stakes."

"Turtle nest stakes?" She sipped her root beer. The bubbles tickled her tongue.

He nodded. "Loggerhead turtles nest from May to October. Sarasota beaches are popular

nesting spots. Storms can wash up the cages or stakes buried in the sand." He used the back of his hand to wipe mustard from his chin. "My friends and I have gone on a few walking tours. You come out to the beach at night, and if you're here at the right time, you might get to watch the mama turtle dig a nest in the sand and lay her eggs."

"I'd love to see that. You said May to October?"

"Yep. Another time I got to see the hatchlings scurry across the sand. The moonlight reflected off the water and guided them home." He gazed at the waves lapping the shore, and his eyes twinkled. "It's the most beautiful scene I've ever seen."

"You sound passionate about—what's the word when you work to save...," she used her hands as if she could wave the word off the tip of her tongue.

"Conservation?"

"That's it—conservation."

"If I didn't have to work construction, I would love to get a job at an aquarium. Maybe continue my education and get a degree—" His voice trailed off and took his excitement with it. "But that's not gonna happen."

"Is this what you meant the other night when we talked about getting baptized in the church?"

He lifted his eyes to meet hers, but he didn't speak a word. He didn't need to—his expression said it all.

"Have you talked to your family?"

"No. Our bishop permits me to volunteer on occasion." He shrugged. "My parents know about it, but..."

The sound of his words led her to conclude this arrangement was not enough to satisfy his soul.

"Though I'm not in the same situation—" She buried her toes deeper into the sand. "I understand how it feels when you don't meet the expectations of others."

"It's a shame when expectations stand in the way of our dreams. What do you dream about?"

"Good question." A memory tied to Josiah surfaced. She struggled to think of another story to share, but her mind went blank. "Since coming to Florida, my answer has changed. But I do know, for certain, that I don't want to disappoint my father. Been there. Done that."

"Nothin' worse than seeing your *daed* wearing a disappointed expression and knowin' you're the one who put it there." He sipped his soda and tilted the bottle toward the water. "Hope Siesta Key hasn't disappointed you."

"Hardly. It's so much better than the pictures on the post-cards."

"And there's so much more to see and do. Think you're up for it?"

CHAPTER EIGHTEEN

Mariah followed Luke at a safe distance as their bikes bounced over the red brick street past brightly colored store-fronts until he rolled to a stop in front of a replica lighthouse.

He pointed to a sign on the door. "I've always wanted to do this but never have."

"Do what?"

He looked at her through wide eyes. "Parasail with me?"

"No way. Absolutely not." She backed away from the door. "I've heard horror stories. And remember what I just said about not disappointing my *daed*?"

"Alrighty then." He gestured toward a picture taped to the window. "Jet skis?"

"Now those are more my speed."

"Speed, you say?" He leaned down a couple of inches and looked in her eyes.

"But not too fast."

"I don't know. I can see it in your eyes—you wanna go fast."

She bit her lip, but her smile gave away her true feelings.

"I knew it." He clapped his hands.

"You shouldn't boast, Luke." She winked and adjusted the beach bag on her shoulder as she entered the rental shop behind him.

At the desk, he flashed his Boaters Safety card to the employee and signed the waiver. She filled out her home address and wrote her name on the line. They each fastened the straps of a life jacket across their chests before joining several others to watch a quick safety video.

Beside her, a young child squirmed in his seat. The boy's sister, who couldn't have been older than ten, looked as calm as a lamb as an employee reviewed what steps to follow in case of an emergency. The open water, still near the horizon, curled into waves like cupped hands waiting to pull her under. Despite the relaxed crowd seated around her, her heart pumped quicker. She scooted closer to Luke on the bench and wiped her palms on her dress.

"Doin' okay?" he whispered. Placing a finger on her jawline, he turned her face toward him, which redirected her focus. "Where'd the spark go?" His eyes flicked back and forth as he searched hers. "This'll be fun. You'll be glad you did it. And you'll be with me. I'll keep you safe." He nudged her with his elbow but left his arm close so they were still touching.

"*I'll keep you safe.*" Her thoughts shifted to Josiah. What would he think about her hanging out with another guy all day? Would he ever ditch his clothes and run into the ocean, wearing only his swim trunks like Luke did? Oh, she shouldn't compare them. She couldn't compare them. She was scheduled to return home soon. Luke would be miles away—with Sarah. Maybe? She shook away her thoughts as the instructors shouted out last-minute safety rules.

Luke stood. "Here we go." He offered her his hand.

Mariah hesitated but then rolled her eyes as she accepted his help off the bench.

He laughed and gathered their belongings. "We can pack these in the storage compartment on the jet ski."

"I can't believe I let you talk me into this."

"You came to Florida for adventure, right?"

She tilted her face toward her shoulder.

"Our construction company motto is 'Restoring the past, Building the future.'"

"Yes, I remember the ad at the post office."

"Days, weeks, even years from now, we'll look back on today, and this will all be a memory. Am I right? Let's make it a good one."

"Building the future," she repeated in a soft voice. This was a perfect opportunity to embrace the adventure. Kids rode jet skis all the time. "You're right. Let's do this."

"I'll drive first, and you can hold on to me." Luke climbed aboard and used his thumb to motion for her to get on behind him. "Once we get out there, I'll let you take control."

To make her dress shorter, she tucked a couple of inches of fabric near her navel into the waistband of her underwear and swung her right leg over the seat. She wrapped her arms around his waist and couldn't help but press her forearms against his hard muscles.

Revving the engine, he slowly pulled away from the dock. Once he was out of the wake zone, he leaned back toward her. "Hold on tight."

She squeezed her arms around his body as the jet ski accelerated, shooting water all around them. The cool spray tickled her bake skin. She squealed with joy as he sped along the coast. Nearing four pontoon boats that had tied together, he slowed the watercraft.

"This is Big Pass. It runs between Siesta Key and Lido Key." He pointed to his right. "There's a big sand bar here. The beaches on Lido Key are eroding. Some say dredging sand from Big Pass is the solution. Others worry about the impact on the water quality and marine life, including the seagrass. It's been a big controversy."

"Sounds like you know a lot about it." She let go of his waist and placed her hands on her thighs. Her dress was soaked with salt water.

"I've read arguments from both sides in the newspaper. To learn more about marine life and conservation, I also borrow a fair share of books from the library."

"I love to read—mostly romances, but I'll pick up a book about any subject."

"Romances, huh?"

A tour group of kayakers emerged from the mangrove tunnels and passed behind a pontoon. They followed each other along the shore like ducklings waddling after their mother.

"I once went on a kayak tour through those mangroves. Incredible sights up close and personal: anemones, star fish, mollusks, crabs. I'd love a job like that."

"That sounds fun." Her voice sounded more enthusiastic than she felt. Her heart ached for her new friend, but she didn't dare encourage him to follow his dreams. It was not her place. She would be leaving Florida soon. He would move on, and memories of their time together would fade into the past and be forgotten.

"Enough about me. Let's switch places." He drove the jet ski closer to the sand bar. Once he had gotten off, she scooted forward. Luke passed the safety lanyard to her, and she tight-ened it around her wrist. He placed his hand on her shoulder and swung his left leg over the seat. The jet ski tipped from side to side as he sidled up to her from behind. She leaned back into him as he reviewed the operating instructions they'd heard on the safety video. He felt familiar—like the way it felt when she danced with Dustin in the field. She blinked away the memories, but she couldn't shake away her thoughts. She enjoyed spending time with Luke, and she felt comfortable and at ease when she was with him. Much like she felt with Josiah.

"Okay. You ready?" He patted her side and wrapped his arms around her waist.

She rolled her neck and looked at him from the corner of her eye. "Are *you* ready?"

He smiled.

After pressing the green button near the left handle, she depressed the throttle with her right hand. "Hang on!" she yelled over the engine as it roared to life. She steered away from the pontoons and headed south toward Siesta Key. When the waves got choppy, she slowed to a cruising speed. Her eyes darted from left to right, and she kept mental notes about the other boaters around her. One guy on a jet ski caught her eye as he spun the watercraft in a half circle. On his next pass, he made a complete revolution and sped off down the beach.

Her eyes widened. "Did you see him? Can we try it?"

Luke laughed. "Whatever you'd like." He tightened his arms around her and locked his wrists.

Her heart thumped as she planned out her route in her mind and then accelerated. When they were in wide open wa-ter, she turned the handlebars to the left and let go of the throttle.

Their screams dissolved into laughter. "Oh my goodness. That was crazy. I wanna do it again."

"Go for it." Luke ran his hands through his hair and then resumed his hold on her.

Mariah steered away from the beach. "Want to try a full circle?"

"Of course."

Though she was a novice, she drove with the confidence of an expert. She gained speed, scanned the scene around her, and pulled the handlebars as far as she could to her right. Instead of releasing the throttle as she had on past runs, she continued to squeeze the handle. The world spun past her eyes. She flew from the jet ski and splashed into the Gulf. The salt burned her eyes, and she gagged when she tasted her first gulp of salt water. Her life jacket kept her bobbing at the surface.

Luke? She glanced to her right and left but didn't see him until she swam closer to the jet ski, which rested upside down in the water. Craning her neck, she caught sight of his bright red lifejacket about 10 yards behind the watercraft.

"Luke!" She fought the wake of a passing ski boat and swam to his side.

He grimaced and plunged his hands below the water.

"Are you okay? I'm so sorry." She reached for his life jacket and held his face above the water.

"I'm fine." He sucked air through clenched teeth. "I slammed my shin on the jet ski when we flew off."

"I didn't know that would happen. I shouldn't have—"

"Mariah." He reached out and touched her cheek. "I'm okay."

She filled her lungs with a deep salty breath.

"I'll have a decent bruise, but working construction, I'm

used to being black and blue." He winked.

"But have you ever flipped?" she lifted her eyebrows.

"I've flown off many times, but I've never flipped." He climbed onto the inverted watercraft and stood on the right side. "My friends have."

"Oh, Luke. Your leg." She covered her mouth with her hand as she stared at the purple goose egg on his shin. "I'm sorry," she said through her fingers.

As he bent forward to grab the jet ski's grate on its left side, he ran his hand over the bump. "That's a *gut* one." He leaned backward, and the jet ski landed with a splash as it slammed into the water.

"I think I'll let you drive now." She wrestled the safety lanyard on her wrist.

"No, I think you need to get back in the saddle, so to speak. Seeing you have fun makes me happy."

The wake from a passing pontoon splashed Mariah's face. She sputtered.

"You okay?" He laughed.

"Nice. I get a mouthful of salt water, and you laugh. Well, I guess it serves me right."

"Don't say that." He swam closer to her. "This has been a great day."

"I've had a lot of fun. I'm glad you invited me to join you."

The water calmed and gently rocked the pair from side to side. He locked eyes with her and didn't look away, then tilted his head toward the jet ski. "Here, I'll help you up."

With her back toward his chest, she prepared to accept a boost. His muscular arms pushed her from the water so she could climb into the seat. The task proved to be more difficult than she had imagined because her long dress stuck to her legs. Once situated, she offered him a hand.

"We should return this rental and get ice on your leg."

"See, you do care about me." The dimple in his left cheek deepened.

CHAPTER NINETEEN

Umbrellas striped in rainbow colors dotted the public beach, and the squeals of children in the gulf waters mingled with the call of the seagulls in the ocean breeze. Though the bruise on his shin looked terrible, Luke suggested they take a walk, and he managed without a limp.

Mariah grabbed a plastic grocery bag blowing across the sand, but she didn't toss it in the nearby garbage can.

"What are you doing?" he asked with a sideways glance.

"I'm going to keep this in case we find any trash. Clean beaches are important to you, so it's important to me."

Taking her hand in his, he then gave a slight squeeze and led her down the beach.

"Thirsty?" He lifted his chin as they approached an open-air snack shack with a thatched roof. "I could go for an ice-cold lemonade right now. You?"

"Lead the way." She motioned for him to move and then followed him along the boardwalk to the shade of a covered patio. Leaning her elbow on an empty high-top table, she rested her chin in her palm and blocked out the hum of con-versation around her. Focusing on the incredible view proved easy. A gentle breeze tussled the palm trees, and the scent of gardenias filled the air around her. To her right, giant white blossoms sprang forth from a row of bushes along the patio.

"Here you go." Luke reappeared and handed her a tall glass topped with a bright blue paper umbrella. "I skipped straws. Turtles can ingest them, and the straws get lodged in their bodies."

"That's awful. I don't need one." She vowed to never use a straw again. Looking out across the sand, she imagined the scene he'd described earlier—the hatchlings scurrying through the darkness in search of the water. In the distance, a wave crashed onto the beach. "Do you get tired of the scenery around here? I mean, do you ever catch your breath because you're surrounded by beauty?"

"I've lived here my whole life. I guess I'm used to it, but I don't think I'm tired of it."

As they continued walking she sipped the lemonade. The tang of sour followed by a burst of sweetness on her tongue caused her lips to pucker. "I'll miss this place."

"I'm sure you're missing home, but I'm glad you're in town for a couple more weeks."

"Three more weeks to be exact."

"Even better. I'd like to spend more time with you."

He wanted to spend more time with her. Her body trem-bled, and warmth rushed up her neck into her cheeks.

Confusion muddied her thoughts. Of course she wanted to return to her family, to her friends, to—how did she feel about seeing Josiah? Had his feelings for her changed since their disagreement, since she'd been gone? How would her feelings for Luke fit into the equation once she settled back into her regular routine?

"The weather here in the winter is so much better than at home. I can't believe the warm sun has already dried my dress." She ruffled the wrinkled fabric with her hands.

"It's mighty hot today. There should be some cover down this way a little further."

Discovering a shady, more secluded spot surrounded by tall ornamental grasses, they unrolled their towels side by side to face the surf. Seagulls called to each other, soaring in the breeze. He removed his shirt and ran to splash water over his neck and shoulders.

Tossing her bag on the ground, she folded the shirt so she wouldn't get caught staring. But she snuck a peek at the hard lines of his upper body. "Ouch." A sharp pain across the ball of her foot forced her to her knees.

"What happened? Step on something?" Luke swiped his hand through the sand. "Look at this—a conch shell."

The spines rose sharp against her fingers. "No wonder it hurt."

"What a great souvenir to take home." Their hands brushed as she accepted the shell from him, yet he didn't pull away. "When you look at it, remember our time together."

"I do have a good time with you, that's for sure." Using her pinky, she wiped the granules of sand from the shell's smooth undersurface and then slid it into her beach bag.

They sat side by side in silence as the waves brought words to mind but then washed away her courage to speak them.

He edged closer to her and lowered his voice. "Um...I must be honest and say what is on my heart, or I will regret it for the rest of my days."

She raised her eyes and met his.

"Mariah, you cause me to think and feel like no woman

I've ever known. I know we've only known each other for a week, but I've shared my hopes and dreams with you, and I haven't spoken those words to anyone else." He interlaced his fingers with hers. "I've grown to care for you. I don't think we crossed paths by chance."

"I—I don't know what to say. What about Sarah? And your family?"

"Sarah's thoughtful and sweet and mighty pretty, but I'm certain she's not the woman I'm supposed to marry. She doesn't stir up a drive in me to be a better man—not the way you do."

Mariah forced her eyes from the beads of water glistening on his broad shoulders and instead focused on the golden flecks in his eyes. "I make you want to be a better man?"

"*Jah*, you do."

Resting her head against his chest, she rubbed her thumbs across his calloused palms. He leaned close and lifted her chin with one finger. His lips brushed against hers, and she closed her eyes, allowing him to envelop her in a strong kiss until she pushed away from him, breathless.

"Mariah, I don't know—I'm sorry. Maybe I shouldn't have done that."

"It's okay." The whispers caught in her throat. "But we should probably—"

Probably what? The sound of her heart thundered in her ears while her mind struggled to keep up. She made him want to be a better man? Did Josiah share this sentiment? If she pursued a relationship with Luke, she'd be saying goodbye to Josiah. The thought brought with it a wave of uncertainty.

Luke put his lips near her ear. "What are you thinking?"

"I don't know." Mariah shook her head. "On one hand, your words make my heart happy. Really happy. On the other hand, I came down here to find myself and figure out who *Gott* created me to be. A relationship with a man—feeling something more than friendship for you—wasn't in the plan."

"For I know the plans I have for you, said the Lord."

"Jeremiah 29:11. One of my favorite scriptures." She paused. "Guess I need time to process all of this."

—

Rinsing the salt water from her skin in a warm shower, refreshed Mariah in both body and mind. She climbed into bed and spread her grandmother's quilt across her lap, then settled against the feather pillow. Heat rushed to her cheeks as she replayed the goodnight kiss in her mind. She had learned a great deal about Luke and his family during their short time together, and she could picture her place in his life.

But how could that be? She crossed her arms over her face. They didn't have the history she shared with Josiah, the secret language that had developed between the two of them over the years—the look he could give her or the random word he could say that brought a memory to the surface, causing her to burst into laughter, and not always at the appropriate times. Her place in his life had already been established, and he'd invited her to be part of his future.

Earlier this evening, before she and Luke had said goodnight, he'd asked her if she wanted to hang out on Friday. She'd still meet him, right?

The bed creaked as she flopped onto her back. Her life and her future needed to be her focus. After all, that was the reason for this trip to Pinecraft.

The quilt's soft squares wrinkled beneath her fingers. Lifting the flap of the next fabric envelope, she wiggled the note from the pocket.

My dearest Mariah,

When I left my parents' house, my friends, and my community to stay with my sister and her family, I struggled through my days. When it got dark and I laid in bed at night, doubts crept into my thoughts. I feared I wasn't meeting the expectations others had of me. At first, I wasn't completely convinced I was going down the path God had set out before me. One day I mustered up the courage to speak with the bishop of my new community. He quoted Proverbs 4:23. "Above all else, guard your heart, for everything you do flows from it."

To this day, I'm thankful for this advice because I followed my heart and married your daadi. I was in love with him, and I treasure the 40 years we spent together. Though I broke my mother's heart when I left, I don't regret my decision to spend my life with this man. I hope this Bible verse offers you encouragement as well.

With love,
Mammi

Mariah held the note to her chest. *Mammi* said to guard her heart. Guard her heart? She was now more confused than ever.

⸺

On Wednesday evening, Mariah entered her aunt's cozy kitchen. Turkey meatballs sizzled in a cast iron pan on the stove, filling the air with smells of oregano and thyme. She stirred the simmering pot of marinara sauce with a wooden spoon.

Aunt Birdie walked through the back door, shuffling a stack of envelopes.

"Hello, dear. You have a letter here." Her aunt placed the note on the island countertop.

"I do? Wonder who it's from."

"There's no return address, but the sender has impressive penmanship."

Josiah.

Mariah recalled the times when their teacher would interrupt class to compliment her friend's cursive. She snatched the letter from the island and raced out of the room.

"Excuse me for a minute, Aunt Birdie," she called over her shoulder.

After shutting and locking the door, she pounced on the bed and tore open the light blue envelope. A two-page letter. She forced her lungs to breathe.

Dear Mariah,

I hope you're enjoying your time in Florida. I realize you'll be home in a couple of weeks. I wasn't going to write, but I decided I want to explain myself and give you time to think about what I have to say before we meet again face to face.

Before you left, I was disappointed, hurt, and angry. I didn't understand why you were looking for love and attention from someone else—especially when the person did not share our faith.

The evening I picked you up and took you home in the snowstorm, I wanted to wrap you in my arms and take your pain away. But I didn't. You needed time and space, and I didn't want to confuse you.

Since you've been gone, I tried to move on—maybe to get even with you, I don't know. I've spent time with another girl I met at a singing. We get along well, but if I'm being honest with myself, there's no future for us. I've considered talking with other girls, but I have no desire. Why? Because my heart loves only you. No one else compares.

When I think about my life, you have always been a big part of it. You've not been gone long, but we hadn't really talked for a couple of months before you left. I miss the sound of your laugh when I attempt to tell a joke. I miss how you tap your toes on the floor under the table like those dancers at the fair. I miss everything about you, and I would go to the ends of the earth to make you happy.

When we spoke after church at the Schrock's farm, I told you I couldn't promise I'd be waiting for you when you figured this all out. I've regretted those words since the moment I spoke them. The day after you'd left, I went out to Pioneer Trails to buy a ticket to come see you—to talk in person, but my brother talked me out of it because I had promised I'd give you space. Instead, I spent some time collecting my thoughts and decided to write to you. When you get home, I will wait and let you approach me about this. If you don't bring it up to me, then I'll know you don't feel the same. My heart will be broken, but I'll understand in time.

With love,
Josiah

Mariah read the last sentence through blurry eyes. Tears dampened her dress, and she tugged at the wet fabric covering her chest.

Had he really considered coming all the way down here to see her? Oh, what she'd give to hear Josiah stumble through a joke, to give him a hug. Here she was, having a fabulous time with another guy under the warm Florida sun while he worked long, hard days in frigid temperatures, regretting the last words he'd spoken to her. How his letter increased her yearning for home, to walk down the hall to get advice from her sisters or cross through the evergreens to talk to Lydia.

Across the room, the lap quilt stretched across the chair. Two letters remained. What wisdom would her grandmother share with her today?

With the note in hand, she climbed into bed and snuggled deep into her pillow.

My dearest Mariah,

When I sat down to write this letter, I said a prayer—as I have for all the others. I feel prompted to share Psalm 139: 23-24 with you.

Search me, O God, and know my heart!
Test me and know my anxious thoughts!
And see if there is any offensive way in me,
and lead me in the way everlasting!

I pray these are the words you need to hear at this moment. I hope they offer you peace and comfort, knowing they are from your Heavenly Father.

With love,
Mammi

Mariah flipped the paper over in her hands. That's it? Returning to the quilt, she stuck her fingers into the fabric envelope in search of a second sheet of paper but found the pocket empty. After rereading the note, she bowed her head. Though she prayed, God felt distant.

Had she ever felt this alone?

CHAPTER TWENTY

On Friday afternoon, Mariah popped one last thumbprint cookie in her mouth and returned the final casserole dish to the cabinet. A knock sounded at the front door. Drying her hands on an apron, she rushed to the foyer and swallowed.

"Luke." She straightened her *kapp*. "Is it already three o'clock?"

"I'm a little early. We finished raising the trusses at the job site but can't start the next phase until Monday. Still waitin' on materials. Plus, I was excited to see you." He brushed her arm with his hand, causing the tiny hairs to stand on end. "I can wait on the porch until you're ready—unless you'd like me to come back?"

"Oh, there's no need for that. Please come in." Mariah escorted him to the living room and then paused in the doorway to the kitchen. A light blue shirt highlighted his sand-colored hair and reminded her of Josiah's eyes...

"I'm glad you were able to get away," he said, pulling her to the present.

"Me too. Only one room is occupied tonight, but the couple won't be back until after dinner, and Aunt Birdie left to play cards with her friends. I've finished the tasks she asked me to do, so I'm free."

"I have a surprise." He hooked both thumbs in his suspenders.

"You do? Can I have a hint?"

He shook his head.

"Not even one teensy little clue?"

The left corner of his mouth curved upward. "Then it wouldn't be a surprise."

"Okay. Give me a minute, and I'll be ready to go."

In the bedroom, she pulled a freshly-laundered dress off a hanger in the closet and held the turquoise fabric to her nose, inhaling the fabric softener Aunt Birdie had her add to the dryer. This fragrance would anchor her memories of the time she spent here in Sarasota.

She slipped into a pair of matching flip-flops and met him by the front door. Reaching for a beach bag on the coat rack, she asked, "Do I need to bring anything special for the big surprise?"

"I've taken care of everything." Luke followed her onto the front porch and closed the door behind him. On the sidewalk, he stopped and faced the yard. "Your aunt's garden looks better since you've come to town."

"It's the fence. I added a fresh coat of whitewash this morning. We have a large garden at home, but I'm sad to say I wasn't blessed with a green thumb." She held out her hands and stared at her palms. A smudge of white paint remained on her pinky.

"I knew you had to have a flaw." Luke laughed and nudged her with his elbow.

As they reached Yoder's parking lot, he gestured for her to sit on a bench. "Mack should be here any minute." He rested his foot beside her and tied his shoe. The hem of his pants lifted with the motion.

"Oh, Luke! Your leg!" The skin—now the color of eggplant and beets—stretched over the knot on his shin. "I'm so sorry. That must be incredibly painful."

"Pssh. I'm fine." He slid into the seat beside her and pressed around the bruise with a finger. "It's mighty tender, I won't lie, but it looks way worse than it is."

A black sedan rounded the corner into the parking lot and pulled to a stop in front of the bench.

Though the sun shone over Pinecraft for a great deal of the day, over the past hour, a layer of gray clouds blew in and blanketed the sky. Maybe reality would prove the meteorologist's prediction for a passing shower incorrect.

—

"You had me fooled." Mariah walked beside Luke along a gravel path. "I saw signs for the aquarium and thought you were taking me there."

"Ah, you did, did you? Good guess." He slid his hand over hers and intertwined their fingers. "That was Plan B, but I think the rain is gonna hold off for us. And I'm relieved I didn't have to cancel our reservation, especially since I know the guy. Built a storage shed for his k—." He covered his mouth. "Oops. Almost let it slip."

Reservation? She forced a smile. Her heart rate increased but not from the physical exertion. She truly enjoyed spending time with him, but their relationship had progressed quickly. Should she tell him confusion continued to cloud her thoughts?

No, she didn't want to ruin this. He went to the trouble of making reservations.

Stop. She should tell him.

But she would only be in town for a couple more weeks. The opportunity would arise, and the timing would be better. Having the conversation now would only ruin the evening, and his excitement was palpable.

Her focus remained on the beautiful growth along the path, no longer gravel but sand. They weaved through the group of people gathered near the water's edge. Yellow, red, and orange kayaks rested under trees or on trailers attached to trucks and sport-utility vehicles.

"Remember the mangrove tour I told you about?" He squeezed her hand. "We're going to explore Lido Key by kayak."

While on the jet ski, she *had* said the tour sounded fun, but at the moment, her nerves didn't agree. It was later in the day. They'd finish before dark, right? Maybe this wouldn't be so bad.

Following the guide's directions, she climbed on trembling legs into the front seat of a yellow tandem kayak. With fingers coiled around the paddle, she held her breath, the kayak rocking back and forth in the water as Luke settled into the seat behind her.

"We'll go right up here and wait for the others. You don't have to worry about steering—that's my job." He paddled them away from the narrow strip of sand—away from safety. Peering into the shallow water surrounding them, tiny jellyfish waved spongy fingers and small crabs snapped hello. As they floated around a bend, a spoonbill waded about forty yards away, sweeping its long, flat bill through the shallow water. Two other couples and a guide, wearing a beige, wide-brimmed sun hat, soon caught up to them, and they paddled into the mangroves.

Beneath a canopy of trees that would save them from a sunburn on a clear day, the twisted roots rose several feet from the water on both sides, creating a narrow tunnel. Birds tweeted from branches above as her paddle smacked against the roots. Luke's encouragement motivated her to keep trying when she wanted to quit.

"You got it. Nice and easy." He maneuvered them through the mangrove tunnels, dipping his paddle into the water, careful not to disturb the vegetation and wildlife living below the surface. "There's a mollusk here," he called to the guide. "May I grab it?"

"Please do." The man held his paddle almost perpendicular to the water to slow his kayak.

She turned her head as Luke pulled up a pearly gray shell surrounding a brown spongy tissue. The brown disappeared, and water sprayed in Luke's face.

Mariah gasped, but Luke laughed, wiping his chin.

"Glad your mouth was closed." The guide reached out for the shell. "When the mollusk shrunk inside the shell to hide, the water it displaced squirted out. Rest assured, this guy wasn't spitting at him." He returned the shell to the water and resumed paddling.

Ten yards later, he slowed and pointed to his right. "Oh, lookie here." He reached beneath the surface and produced a starfish as dark as pecans, dotted with cashew-colored spots. Its points stretched to cover the majority of his palm. "Would you care to hold it?" His arm extended toward her.

"Not this time." She clutched the paddle near her chest.

"You should. The little hairs on the undersurface tickle." Luke's gentle tone could not persuade her.

"I'm good."

Once the others had a chance to hold the starfish, Luke placed it on a root beneath the water. Her confidence with the paddle increased when they left the mangroves and she didn't have tight turns to consider. Her nerves calmed in the peaceful surroundings.

Luke whispered, "Look up! It's an osprey." The bird circled with impressive wings outstretched. Hovering high above the water, it dove feet-first, and snatched a fish with its talons.

Her mouth hung open as the powerful predator disappeared into the trees. She twisted to say something, her movement rocking the kayak in the still water. Instead she faced forward and shook her head as they paddled after the group into the bay.

"We'll spend the remainder of our time here in the bay." The guide gestured toward the open water. "That's Siesta Key you see there to our right, and Bird Key is off to the left. The sun will set soon. Maybe we'll see a manatee or a dolphin."

The sun will set soon? Shouldn't they start heading back to shore? Muscles throughout her body contracted as the group of kayaks traveled further from the land. The low clouds darkened the water around them, and blood rushed to her ears.

What had the guide said? Evidence of a manatee? Where? Here?

Chewed stalks of sea grass floated between the kayaks. While she enjoyed viewing the gentle giants behind glass, the thought of a sea cow lurking in the water beneath their kayak sent her heart into spasms.

As she tried to control her breathing, the four kayaks formed a line facing west, and the other tourists held up their phones to capture the sun's descent. The dark water resembled black volcanic rock, the sun spilling over the horizon like molten lava, and the puffy, gray clouds a warning signal of an imminent eruption. Her body relaxed enough for her mind to appreciate the beauty.

A fin appeared to her right, slicing through the water without making a sound. The scream stuck in her throat like a mollusk tucked within a shell.

"A dolphin!" Luke's movement caused the kayak to teeter. Cameras switched subjects as the dolphin reappeared—this time so close she could have touched it with her paddle, if she weren't petrified.

They waited longer than she liked for the dolphin to make another appearance, but then ran out of time. "Turn your headlamp on, Mariah," Luke said. Her silhouette stretched across the water in the glow of his light.

She managed to press the button. Even more terrified to kayak by flashlight, she squeezed her eyes shut and pretended to paddle to shore. As soon as she braced her arms against the sides, Luke stepped into the shallow water and pulled the kayak onto the sand. Her legs shook as she climbed onto dry land.

"That was incredible!" He lifted her and twirled around, setting her back on the ground. "I loved every single minute of that trip. What was your favorite part?"

This. Getting out of the boat.

Instead of speaking her mind, she said, "The sunset. I've never seen such a beautiful sight." At least that was the truth.

They walked hand-in-hand up the gravel incline toward the parking lot past trucks and trailers holding kayaks and life vests. She took a deep breath and allowed her neck and shoulders to relax. When they reached the pavement, a light sprinkle tickled her bare arms.

"Nice." Luke held his free palm to the sky. "Well, it has held off all day, ain't so?"

Nodding, she continued to struggle with the guilt and dishonesty battling within her. Maybe she should ask to return to the B&B, in case he had another surprise.

The rain fell harder, and they quickened their steps. She welcomed the shower, first dropping Luke's hand and then extending her arms. When was the last time she played in the rain? She closed her eyes against another memory of Josiah as it swirled to mind. Twirling, she opened her mouth and giggled. The cold drops of rain tickled her tongue.

Luke grasped her waist and they danced a few steps before he stopped her. Standing face to face, their eyes locked. She melted into his strong arms and allowed him to kiss her neck. His lips traveled up to her ear and then down to her collarbone. He brushed her cheek with his thumb and graced her lips with a gentle kiss. Despite her confusion, she did not tire of his touch.

"I wish you didn't have to leave," he whispered in her ear.

The rain dripped off his straw hat and trickled down his face. His shirt was soaked, and she could see the hard lines of his shoulders and chest through the thin fabric. She ran her hands over his muscles and locked her wrists around his neck, giving him a long squeeze.

Stepping back, she lifted her chin. His eyes searched hers. "I've shared pieces of myself with you that I wouldn't dream of telling another soul. Until now. With you." He reached for her hands. "I love you."

"Oh, Luke. I can't." She paused and filled her lungs with the smell of the damp earth, masking the scent of his soap.

"You love me? How? We've not known each other for very long."

"That is true. But I knew I loved you the day I drove by the B&B, and you were weeding with your dress tucked—"

"Okay. Please stop." She covered her face with her hands. "I need a minute."

"Why? I got the feeling you felt the same way about me?"

"I'm confused. My feelings for you are real, but at the same time this is all so surreal. It's like I'm living in a movie."

"I hope it's a movie with a happy ending."

She turned away.

"Don't tell me there's someone else?"

"There is," she whispered.

He squinted his eyes as if to understand her hesitation. "Has he, like me, told you he loves you?"

She nodded.

With an audible exhalation, he hung his head and rubbed the back of his neck. "I can't believe this."

"But I'm not sure how I feel about my relationship with him either. It's complicated." The tension in her temples eased beneath her fingers. "I don't know how I got into this situation. I have so many questions and so little time."

"Like what?" He led her to the shelter, and they sat next to each other at a picnic table.

"When I go home, what do you see happening between us?"

"To be honest, I hadn't thought that far ahead. I guess I thought we could write to each other. Maybe you could visit again? Maybe I could take the bus up to see you?"

"But I mean farther down the line. Say we're together seven years from now. Where do you see yourself? Us?"

He stayed quiet for several minutes. From a low branch, a

bird swooped under a nearby table. She kicked a pebble into the grass.

"I see myself here in Sarasota," he said. "I enjoy my job, and I don't want to leave the Gulf. You've inspired me to get more involved in conservation efforts, if our bishop allows me to pursue my dreams, within reason, that is. I would love for you to be by my side, with a bunch of *kinner* running around our legs." He linked his pinky with hers.

"You've painted a pretty picture. In this scenario, I would need to leave my family and friends to move here to be with you. We met two weeks ago. It's not that I don't care for you—it's all happening so fast."

"It is."

"I definitely have a lot to consider."

"And you leave soon. I wish we had more time together to sort through our feelings."

This trip was supposed to help her clear her head. Instead, she held yet another man's heart in her hands.

CHAPTER TWENTY-ONE

Relieved to see a light burning from the crack under Aunt Birdie's bedroom door, Mariah crept through the dark hallway. After one knock, the older woman answered.

"Mariah?" She swung the door open and pulled her terry cloth robe tight around her wide waist. "Is everything okay?"

"Can we talk? Is—is it too late?" Her eyes darted around the room for signs her aunt was ready to go to bed.

"Of course we can talk, my dear. Please come in." Aunt Birdie shuffled to the bed and slid a bookmark in her novel. Placing the book next to a cup of tea on her nightstand, she patted the mattress. "Sit beside me."

Despite her efforts to take a seat with care, Sunny stirred from his slumber at the foot of the bed. Mariah rubbed between his ears, and he drifted back to sleep. "I—I don't know where to begin. It's complicated, and I'm confused."

"Well, as Maria says in the *Sound of Music*, 'Let's start at the very beginning. A very good place to start.'" Her aunt sang the words to the song Mariah had loved as a child. "It worked for her."

She gathered her long hair in a bun and then let it spill over her shoulders as she forced the air from her lungs. "On my birthday, my friend Josiah told me he loved me, and he asked if he could court me."

"Is that so?"

"I know, you're probably wondering, if that's the case, why have I been spending so much time with Luke?"

"I'm not wondering anything, dear. Just listening."

"Josiah's one of my best friends, but...I'm not sure if I'm to spend my future with him. I'm not sure about my future at all." Mariah allowed her focus to fall to the quilt, hexagonal pieces of fabric sewn into flowers in shades of carnation pink and rose. "I snuck out to a couple parties and spent some time with a guy named Dustin. He's not Amish. Josiah was angry with me, especially when I got into trouble and the police had to drive me home in the middle of the night."

"I see." Aunt Birdie sipped her tea.

"The officer gave me a warning, but it didn't make the experience any less scary, that's for sure. I embarrassed myself and my family. And then, to top it all off, I learned Dustin was involved with someone else." She hung her head. "He really hurt me."

"I imagine he did."

"After all of that, *Mammi* arranged this trip for me so I could have some time and space to find some answers, to figure it all out." She paused and wrung her fingers. "Then you introduced me to Luke."

"Yes."

"And he's incredible. We enjoy being together, and we've had deep conversations—we've shared our hopes and dreams. He's told me how he feels about me—about us—"

"But—"

"But to have a future with him, I'd have to leave Holmes County— leave my home—to live here. It sounds crazy to even consider because it's all happening so fast. I'm leaving soon with more questions than when I arrived, and I don't know what to do or say to anyone."

Aunt Birdie wrapped an arm around her shoulders. "That is quite a predicament." She sat silent for a moment. "As for the boys, you need to tell them both the truth. There's nothing wrong with telling them you're confused. Time and distance will sort out your heart."

"What do you mean?"

"You'll soon see. When you're back home, are you missing Luke? Do you want to be with him? Can you picture leaving Berlin and moving to Pinecraft? Can you imagine yourself in his life? And with Josiah, ask yourself those same questions. The answers will soon be clear. And who knows, maybe you're not supposed to be with either of them."

"Great." Mariah rested her forehead in her palm. "You've got to be kidding me."

Her aunt chuckled. "My experience differs from yours, but I know how it feels to disappoint others. Would you care to hear my story?"

"Please." She shifted in her seat on the bed.

"Growing up, I never doubted that I would get baptized in the Amish church." The woman crossed her ankles and cinched the robe near her chest. Her voice lowered. "During my *Rumspringa*, I was assaulted and got pregnant. I hid the pregnancy from my family and friends for the first few months, but then I miscarried."

Mariah muffled a gasp with her hand.

"I was angry with how people in my community—and some members of my family—treated me afterward. I had not asked for any of this to happen. I'm still not sure why, but God allowed me to experience the suffering. And then He led me to George, God rest his soul." She picked up a silver picture frame from the nightstand.

A man with a round face, square chin smiled from behind the glass. "I think *Mammi's* told us stories about him. He's handsome."

"This man loved me until the day he died." She traced her finger along the curve of his shoulder. "About a month after we met, I knew I wanted to be with him. But pursuing a relationship with him meant I had to abandon my desire to get baptized in the Amish church."

"I imagine it was a difficult decision to make." Mariah propped her feet on the bedframe. What if she had turned from her faith to be with Dustin? What if she had to say goodbye to her family to pursue a life with the man she loved? "Heartbreaking."

"Oh, it certainly was. As a result, I struggled for a long time with my identity. For years, in fact."

"You're such a strong, independent woman. How did you get over it?"

"I'm not sure I got over it, but I did move past it through prayer, and I surrounded myself with people who encouraged me, leaving behind those who tried to drag me down. Over time, God showed me I didn't have to work off my past sins. I was not a failure. Instead, I was wanted and loved by Him."

Sneaking out to parties and pursuing Dustin had proved to be a poor decision. Mariah filled her lungs and then blew the air through puffy cheeks, releasing her regret.

"We ladies are not defined by our past mistakes or by our relationships. Whether Amish or not, society tries to tell a different story." Aunt Birdie returned the frame to the nightstand. "What are you thinking?"

"I'm gonna miss being here."

"I'm going to miss having you around here. You're welcome to visit any time. My door is always open." Aunt Birdie wrapped her in a tight embrace. "And as for those boys, remember: truth and time."

Mariah closed her bedroom door as the grandfather clock chimed for the eleventh time. Though morning would not wait, she unfolded the final letter from her grandma and skimmed the carefully scripted words.

My dearest Mariah,

There's a saying that goes, "Some people come into your life for a reason, some a season, and some a lifetime." While you've been in Pinecraft, you may have made new friends who you may never see again, but you have crossed paths with them for a reason. Others you may stay connected with once you get home, but due to time and distance, your relationship dwindles. Still others will be close for a lifetime. I'm reminded of Philippians 1:3 "I thank God every time I remember you." Praise God for your relationships—for the people who love you as well as for the people who hurt you. Be thankful for the gifts you have received from them. I hope this time in Florida has been the gift you needed. I can't wait to give you a big hug!

Love,
Mammi

She straightened the conch shell on the dresser and then settled into bed. Her eyelids grew heavy as she composed a letter to Josiah in her head.

CHAPTER TWENTY-TWO

"Mariah, dear? It's time to get going." Aunt Birdie's voice sounded through the bedroom door.

"Just a minute." She dotted the *i* in Josiah and slipped the paper into the top dresser drawer. The letter would have to wait.

"Mariah. Now!"

"Coming." She slid her feet into flip-flops and rushed into the kitchen as Aunt Birdie secured Sunny in his cage. "Ready."

"Good. I need to get to the park early. The ladies and I want to be there to greet the ministry road team. We're expecting a big turnout. Everyone will be there."

"Everyone?" Mariah cringed. Please not Sarah. Somehow she'd managed to avoid her since meeting her at the park.

"I mean, who doesn't love big pretzels and ice cream?" Her aunt wiped the island countertop with a paper towel.

"Your group sure knows how to bring in a crowd." Mariah unwrapped a mint and popped it in her mouth.

"Grab the bag with the quilt for me, would ya? It's by the

front door. I'll meet you on the sidewalk."

Mariah peeked in the bag. Aunt Birdie spent every minute of free time over the past week finishing the adorable quilt. The faces of nine caramel-colored teddy bears were stitched to lavender and violet fabric squares. Her favorite bear wore a pair of eyeglasses. This quilt would raise a good deal of money in today's silent auction.

She crossed the street beside her aunt, and they walked to Pinecraft Park. Dixie and Luke stood near their parents by one of four folding tables set up in the silent auction area. Large rocks held the bidding papers in place. Mariah waved.

Aunt Birdie pointed to a clothesline strung between two trees. "Hang that quilt over there for me, next to the green and burgundy monkey wrench. I saw the ministry team's van pull into the parking lot."

Mariah crossed the grassy area and unfolded the teddy bear quilt and reached for a clothespin.

"Here, let me help you." The scent of sawdust reached her before he did. "Your aunt make this?" Luke secured one corner to the line.

"She did. I love this guy." The bear wearing eyeglasses smiled back at her. "What'd your family bring for the silent auction?"

"We're offering to build a storage shed for the highest bidder."

They weaved between rocking chairs, bed frames, curio cabinets, and a golf cart. Mariah stopped beside a table covered with quilted goods. "My friend Nora sews pot holders and aprons like these. Maybe we could host a benefit for this prison ministry back home."

"I think I read they're based somewhere in the Midwest.

This team travels around the country, raising money for Bibles and Bible study courses for prison inmates."

"I'll have to talk with our bishop when I get home. I'm sure my family would donate baked goods for the event."

"Sounds like you've got it figured out." His tone of voice didn't change, but a crease appeared between his eyes.

They joined his parents, Dixie, and Aunt Birdie next to a table of baskets.

"Have you enjoyed your time in Pinecraft, Mariah?" Mrs. Yoder scribbled a bid on a sheet.

"*Jah.* I've loved working at the B&B. Aunt Birdie has been gracious and allowed me to get out and have some fun while I've been here." She snuck a peek at Luke. "And the best part is that I'll be here for two more weeks."

He smiled and linked his pinky with hers.

"I told her I was gonna miss her." Aunt Birdie patted her shoulder. "It's been such a pleasure having her in town. We need to get your next trip scheduled on the calendar."

"Yes, we do." Luke drew the attention of the others, and his ears turned red.

"There are the girls." Dixie stood on tiptoe and waved them over.

Mariah snuck sideways glances over her shoulder. Would she have to dodge stares from Sarah this evening? When Luke's admirer wasn't found, Mariah released the breath she'd been holding and muttered a quick prayer of thanks.

The space between the tables grew crowded, and Mariah estimated the lines for big pretzels and ice cream to be forty people deep. The rhythmic plucking of a banjo accompanied a fiddle and a guitar, and a twangy voice belted out lyrics about a man and his hound dog.

While listening to the ministry's team message, she helped

Aunt Birdie collect the bidding papers and record the winners' names. Like Pinecraft, her community could generate a great deal of money for this prison ministry. She'd mention her idea to host a benefit at home in her note to Josiah.

Luke walked up behind the woman who won the teddy bear quilt. "May I walk you home, Mariah?"

"Of course." She pushed her chair away from the table and rose. "I'll see you at home, Aunt Birdie."

Her aunt waved and returned to the conversation with the winner about the quilt pattern she had used.

A couple blocks from the B&B, Luke stopped walking. "I don't want our evening to end."

"We didn't get to spend much time together since I was helping with the silent auction."

"Could we sit here and talk for a few minutes?"

"Yes, we need to talk." She smoothed her dress beneath her legs as she took a seat and placed her purse on her lap.

Luke sat close and put his arm around her. She leaned against his chest. Fuchsia and coral

clouds streaked the sky as the sun dipped below the horizon. The colors reminded her of the conch shell.

She took a deep breath and exhaled slowly. "Luke."

"Mariah?" He tipped his head toward her.

"I've been thinking a lot about us. And praying—" She twisted her fingers.

Luke took her hands in his. "And?"

"When I head home..." She sat silent for a moment.

"Yes."

"You're going to be here." She waited to continue until a woman had passed by them on the sidewalk. "You were right when you said we crossed paths for a reason. And you were right about the kiss."

"Kiss-*es*."

"Kiss-*es*," she repeated and turned to hide her hot cheeks. "But—" She blew out her breath.

"But? You're killing me."

"But over the past few days, I've realized my purpose in your life may be to show you what your future could be like. Sarah may not be the one for you, but I don't think I am either."

He hung his head.

She touched his chin, and his eyes raised to meet hers. "I saw you come alive when you spoke of marine life conservation. You need to be here—where the bishop may allow you to pursue those passions. I need to return to Holmes County and find my own."

"But what about the feelings we've shared for each other?"

"They're real, for sure. But when I spoke with Aunt Birdie last night to help collect my thoughts, she asked me to consider a future with you. Every time I tried to picture our life together, my thoughts kept drifting to Josiah. I'm sorry."

Luke released her hands and leaned forward on his elbows. He pinched the bridge of his nose.

"I didn't know this would happen. I didn't know this is how I would feel." She spoke in a voice above a whisper. "I'm attracted to you, and I care for you, but I don't love you."

When she placed her hand on his back, he straightened.

"Earlier today," she continued. "I was reminded of a Bible verse, Philippians 1:3. 'I thank God every time I remember you.' Luke, I will never forget our time together."

"Nor will I."

A tear ran down her cheek, and he wiped it away with his thumb. Leaning over, he kissed her on the forehead and held her until the street lights came on. "I guess it's time I get you home."

She pushed away from him and rose from the bench.

He took her hand in his and led her the rest of the way home. They climbed the porch steps, and silence stretched between them.

"The B&B's completely booked next week. I'll be busy helping Aunt Birdie, so I don't know if you'll see me around."

"Probably best if we don't see each other anyway."

"You're probably right."

He pulled her close and kissed her forehead. "Take care."

"You too." She waited to enter the house until his shadow disappeared beyond the glow of the streetlight.

The door closed with a soft click, and she rested her forehead on the freshly stained wood. The tears didn't wait for privacy. She'd made the right decision, but she grieved the loss of someone special.

Shuffling slippers approached from behind, and she dried her cheeks with a quick swipe of a sleeve.

"Mariah?" Aunt Birdie wore an apron so she'd been working in the kitchen and not waiting up for her. "I'm so glad you're home. We need to talk."

"Please don't think I'm rude, but it's been a really long day. I think I'd like to turn in. Could this wait until morning?"

"I'm afraid not, dear. Your grandmother called." The lines across her forehead deepened.

"Is everything okay?"

"Let's move into your bedroom, shall we?" Her aunt started down the hall, leaving her no choice but to follow. She closed the door behind them. "Sit."

"I can't." Her knuckles cracked as she wrung her fingers. "What's wrong?"

"There's been an accident. It's not good."

"What happened? Who?"

Moisture collected in the corners of her aunt's eyes.

"Please tell me—who?"

"Josiah."

Her legs buckled at the sound of his name. She fell to the hardwood, bruising her knees.

CHAPTER TWENTY-THREE

Hooking elbows underneath her arms, Aunt Birdie lifted Mariah from the floor. "Come, dear. Lie here on the bed. I'll get you a wet washcloth."

Mariah climbed across the covers and rested her head against the pillow. Phlegm coated her throat, choking each attempt to breathe.

Her aunt returned with a box of tissues and the washcloth as promised.

She blew her nose and then dropped back into the bed. The damp cloth soothed her swollen eyes. "Is it possible to get dehydrated from crying?"

Aunt Birdie chuckled as she reached over and pried the hair loose from her sticky cheeks.

"Would you mind repeating what you said? I heard bits and pieces, but—"

"Of course. I imagine the news was overwhelming to hear. Josiah has settled into the house next door to his parents' farm. He was working in the barn, replacing rotted floorboards in the loft. He must've fallen down the stairs. His brother found him unresponsive on top of his tool box. Paramedics rushed him to the hospital. That's all we know. I'm so sorry."

An image of Josiah lying face down on a dirty barn floor brought bile to the back of her throat. She swallowed hard. Her eyes settled on the dresser drawer where the unwritten letter remained. Instead of writing to tell Josiah she loved him and wanted to spend her life with him, she was at a party, laughing with friends, and resting in the arms of another man. Now a future with her best friend—the man she loved—hung in question. Numbness spread throughout her body. She stared straight ahead, paralyzed by the thought of losing him.

"Tomorrow afternoon, I want you to pack your bags. I'm sending you home."

Mariah pushed onto her elbows and struggled to a seated position. "But Aunt Birdie. You are swamped next week. I came here to help you."

"The bus leaves on Monday at three-thirty."

"But I see how you limp around on that bad knee. I can't leave you. Not even now. How will you manage?"

Her aunt placed a palm against her cheek. "My sweet girl. Your heart for others is what I love most about you. I'll be fine. I've already called Mrs. Yoder. Dixie is going to come to help me. Now, you get some rest. I will need your helping hands tomorrow until you leave, but only if you're feeling up to it. If not, I'll call one of the ladies from my tea group."

"No, I'll be fine."

"Get some sleep. Your Josiah is in my prayers." Aunt Birdie gave her a hug, and Mariah held on until the woman let go. Her aunt turned out the light as she backed through the door.

Your Josiah.

Grief swelled from deep within, her arms and legs heavy against the mattress. Mariah muffled her sobs in her pillow.

———

After another restless night of sleep, Mariah woke on Monday morning to the sound of clattering dishes. She rolled over and saw the big red numbers on the alarm clock. She had overslept again. Jumping from the bed, she hurried to look presentable. Aunt Birdie expected her to help serve breakfast to the guests.

With tendrils of hair peeking from her *kapp*, Mariah rushed into the kitchen. "I'm sorry I overslept." She tied the strings of her apron behind her back.

"No worries, dear. How did you sleep?"

"Not well." She yawned.

"After our conversation on Saturday night, I figured as much. You'll have time to sleep on the bus."

"I'm not so sure about that."

Aunt Birdie passed a large silver tray to Mariah. "Would you please arrange these lemon poppy seed muffins on this platter?"

As she set the last muffin in place, the doorbell rang.

"And could you get that?" With her hands in oven mitts, Aunt Birdie tended to a casserole. "My hands are full at the moment."

Mariah jogged to the front door and swung it open. Luke peeked around a bouquet of gardenia blooms. "What are you doing here?"

"I came to give you these."

"They're gorgeous. You are so thoughtful, but...but why? I thought I was pretty clear—" Her voice trailed off when the fragrance hit her nose, reminding her of their day at the beach and the gardenias at the snack shack with the thatched roof.

"Oh, you were. Crystal clear. But I thought a lot about what you said the other night. And while I didn't want to accept it at first, the morning brought with it a new perspective."

She tilted her head. "How so?"

"Mariah, who's at the door?" Aunt Birdie appeared in the foyer. "Oh, Luke. Good morning. What beautiful flowers." When she bent to smell the bouquet, she got yellow pollen on the tip of her nose.

Mariah laughed and rubbed the smudge with her thumb. "Let me get that for you."

An older couple visiting from New Hampshire descended the stairs. "Good morning, Mr. and Mrs. Franklin. Please be seated in the dining room. Breakfast will be served soon." Aunt Birdie extended her arm to guide them in the right direction.

Mr. Franklin nodded. He placed his hand in the small of his wife's back as they disappeared into the dining room. As Mariah witnessed this loving gesture, she imagined Josiah and his tender touch. Would she get the chance to—? Blinking back tears, she pinched the inside of her arm—the physical pain a distraction from the emotional hurt.

"I'm sorry to interrupt you two," Aunt Birdie said, backing down the hall, "but I could really use your help in the kitchen, dear."

"I won't keep her." When her aunt was out of earshot, he continued. "My mom told me what happened at home. I'm truly sorry."

She stepped into his outstretched arms, placing her head on his chest. A pinch couldn't help her this time, and her tears dampened his shirt. "*Danke*."

"Well, I know you've got a full house." He lowered his arms and kissed her cheek. "I'll keep your friend in my prayers."

As he walked down the steps, she closed the door and whispered, "I will thank *Gott* every time I remember you."

She slipped into the bathroom to wash her face. Her reflection in the mirror stared back at her, and the circles under her eyes reminded her of a lighter version of Luke's bruised shin. What she wouldn't give to use Lydia's concealer and face powder . . .

In the kitchen, Aunt Birdie dished a healthy portion of breakfast casserole on a plate. "Are you okay, dear?"

"Please keep me busy today."

"That won't be a problem." Her aunt handed her a bowl of fruit and a serving spoon. "Would you fill these bowls with fruit? Then we'll be ready to serve."

With glass dishes arranged on a wooden tray, Mariah filled them with melon balls, pineapple, strawberries, and green grapes. She followed her aunt into the dining room where they interrupted a low hum of conversation.

"We understand you're heading back to Ohio today, Mariah." Mrs. Franklin peeled her muffin from its wrapper.

She warmed Mr. Franklin's mug with fresh coffee. "*Jah.* The bus leaves later this afternoon."

"I bet you'll miss this place." The woman sipped her ice water.

Glancing across the table at her aunt, Mariah smiled. "For sure. But I'm anxious to get home."

Aunt Birdie reached between guests to clear a place setting. "I'm gonna miss her. I've gotten used to having her helping hands around this place." Aunt Birdie winced and rubbed her right knee. "But I'm sending her home early. She's excited to get back to see a certain young man." Her voice rose as she raised her eyebrows.

"I see." Mrs. Franklin nudged her husband and winked at Mariah.

Warmth rushed up her neck and into her cheeks. She rounded the table and met her aunt near the buffet. "Has anyone called with an update?"

"I'm afraid not."

What had the doctors learned? Was Josiah in pain? Was he still alive? What if he didn't survive the fall? Was that why nobody had called? She cracked her knuckles and then busied herself by doing the dishes.

The hallways filled with laughter as guests resumed their previous conversations about dining and shopping at St. Armands Circle and trips to the beach. She carried the vase of gardenias to her bedroom and placed them on the dresser next to her conch shell. Unfolding the lap quilt, she admired the fabric envelopes. Lifting the seven flaps, she inspected each pocket, ensuring the treasured letters from her grandma were safe inside. With the conch shell safe inside the folds of the quilt, she slid the bundle into the bag she planned to keep by her side during the bus ride home.

She packed her suitcase and then selected a gardenia from the vase. Knowing the petals may bruise, she slipped the stem into the bag beside the quilt, careful not to damage the bloom. The flower represented the personal and spiritual growth she had experienced while in town, and she wanted to keep this physical reminder. She would remember her time in Pinecraft with fondness, but she couldn't wait to get home.

CHAPTER TWENTY-FOUR

The bus ride from Pinecraft to Berlin proved to be the longest 21 hours of her life. Why hadn't anyone called to give her an update on Josiah before she boarded the bus? Certainly they knew something by now. Unaware of his current condition, she stared out the window, her body paralyzed once again by numbness. The next minute, she locked the bathroom door and gulped for air between sobs as if drowning in her grief. Trapped in this bus, she had no way of knowing how he was doing. Would she get home in time to tell him she'd had a change of heart?

To distract the negative spiral of thoughts, she prayed that she wasn't too late. Returning to her seat, she then flipped through the pages of a magazine and skimmed an article. "Everything You Need to Know About Canning:" canning methods, recipes, equipment, labels, and resources. If the process was as simple as the magazine's name claimed, why did they need this many pages? She made a mental note to pass the issue along to Lydia.

The bus rolled into the German Village Center as she finished reading the page describing how to preserve blueberry jam.

Home sweet home.

Rays from the afternoon sun reflected off banks of snow. Squinting to allow her eyes to adjust to bright white, she slipped on her black bonnet and cinched her coat. As she stepped off the Pioneer Trails bus, she located her grandmother who stood beside their driver near the entrance to the market. Grandma leaned against the coin-operated newspaper racks and sipped her coffee. When she spotted Mariah across the parking lot, she rustled the driver's newspaper with excitement and took a careful step over a puddle toward the car.

Mariah wheeled her suitcase to a stop near the car's rear bumper. "*Mammi!*" She embraced the woman who returned the squeeze for a few moments longer than usual. "I missed you *so* much."

With tears in her eyes, Grandmother beamed. "I'm glad you're home."

Her mother's dress swished as she rushed to give her a hug, and her father wrapped a strong arm around her shoulders and kissed her on the forehead. He didn't speak a word, but by the look in his eyes, it was no secret she had been missed.

"How's Josiah?" Mariah asked. "I've been worried sick."

"That Josiah," her grandmother shook her head. "I hear he's anxious for you to return."

"He's alive?" The words escaped with the breath she'd been holding.

"Oh, goodness gracious. Yes, dear. He's got a concussion and a few broken ribs, but he'll be back on his feet in no time."

She clutched her chest as fresh tear ran down her cheeks.

The driver met them near the trunk and slid her suitcase into place beside the insulated cooler. "How was your trip? Looks like you got a little color."

"Maybe so, but I received *gut* news that brought tears to my eyes."

He patted her on the shoulder. "Glad to have you back."

Climbing into the car behind Carl, she buckled her seatbelt. He started the engine and pulled onto the main road.

"Let's just say I learned a lot, and I'm glad to be home." She smiled and peeked inside her bag to check on the gardenia bloom. The smile turned into a frown when she discovered the petals had faded to a dusty brown.

"*Danke, Mammi*, for arranging this trip for me. And the quilt..." She wiped her eyes with the sleeve of her coat. "Your notes helped me stay focused on *Gott* when times got tough. It was crazy how the note I chose to read was the right note at the perfect time."

"He has a way of meeting us where we are."

"That's for sure." They rounded the bend, and Mariah caught a glimpse of the Weaver farm through the window over her grandmother's shoulder.

The car turned down the next driveway, and Carl shifted into park near Josiah's new home. "Here you are."

"Go on, dear." Her grandmother patted her hand.

"No need to rush home." Her mother touched her forearm. "I want to hear all about your time in Pinecraft, but it's important you visit with Josiah."

Father twisted in the passenger seat to face her. "*Jah*. He's been through quite an ordeal. We'll wait for you to eat dinner."

Mariah stepped from the car and smoothed the dress over her lap. She grabbed a tissue from her coat pocket and wiped her face as if the gesture could remove the puffiness from her eyes and the effects of little sleep.

Her father rolled down the passenger door window. "You look beautiful, *dochder*."

Warmth rose to her cheeks. Though strange to part from her family after her return from a long trip, she lifted her dress and trekked through the snow to the front door.

Mrs. Weaver answered her knock and greeted her with a warm embrace. "Oh, Mariah, dear. It's *wunderbaar* to see you."

"I didn't expect to see you here."

"I brought over some freezer meals that will hold him over until he's up to cooking again. I know he's been awaiting your return. He's supposed to be resting, but I guarantee he's out in the fields checking on those alpacas."

⸺

Heading behind the house, Mariah crossed the yard and entered the barn. Pausing in the open doorway, her eyes adjusted to the darkness. Bean approached, the tapping of his hooves on the concrete floor bounced off the metal roof.

Repetitive scraping on the ground drew her attention to her right. She turned the corner and found Josiah, mucking a stall with one arm. His navy coat hung over the other arm, secured to his side by a sling.

Though she could run to him, hug him, and tell him she loved him, her feet remained cemented to the ground. After all he'd been through, would he be excited to see her? Words scattered in her mind, leaving her at a loss. What should I say? Where should I start?

Bean sauntered over to her and nudged her until she gave in and pet him between the ears. While inhaling the familiar smells, she prayed. As she leaned against the door, a squeak echoed through the cavernous space.

Josiah turned and dropped his pitchfork. "Mariah!" He paused and lowered his voice.

"I'm so sorry."

"You got my letter."

She nodded and allowed the corners of her mouth to curve into a smile.

He limped to her side and wrapped her in an embrace, burying his face in her shoulder. "You came." Her hair muffled the sound. He stepped back and took her hands. "Does this mean...?" His blue eyes twinkled.

"I missed you, Josiah. While I was away, I realized I couldn't picture a future without you. And when I heard about your accident, I thought I was too late. I thought you—"

"Shh. Don't." He shook his head. "I want to move forward."

"Me too. With you." Bean pushed his way between them. "With the alpacas, if you're still—"

He stopped her words with his lips, soft and velvety. She parted her lips, allowing him to deepen his kiss, which sent pulses of pleasure to her curled toes.

He wrapped her in his arms again. "I'm glad you're home." When they stepped apart, he winced.

"What did the doctors say?"

"That I should take it easy."

"Take it easy? They obviously don't know my Josiah." She laughed.

"My Josiah? I like the sound of that. I have a couple chores to finish here in the barn. When I'm through, would you like to go for a ride with me?" He lifted his chin toward the courting buggy parked in the far corner.

"I would love to." She grabbed a broom from a peg on the wall. "And I want you to take a break. Tell me what to do, and I'll help."

After mucking the other three stalls and filling the feed bins for the ten alpacas, Mariah hitched Pete to the buggy. She climbed beside Josiah and snapped the reins. The black Standardbred obeyed and pulled them into the sunlight. She straightened a wool blanket across their laps and snuggled closer to Josiah.

As they plodded past their neighbors' farms in silence, a diesel engine roared behind them. The buggy quaked as the truck passed. Josiah cringed, bracing for a rock that was never thrown. Mariah recognized Dustin's truck. If she had never experienced the thrill of his attention or the heartbreak that followed, would she and Josiah have ended up together anyway? She chose to believe it was God's will.

She squeezed Josiah's arm and rested her head on his shoulder. "I'm ready to begin our future together."

"So am I, and I'll remember this day for the rest of my life," he whispered.

She closed her eyes and said a prayer. Luke was right all along. "You know, days, weeks, even years from now, we'll look back on this day, and it will all be a memory."

"Thanks to *Gott*, this was a good one."

ABOUT THE AUTHOR

While writing Amish fiction and contemporary romance, Laurie Stroup Smith strives to connect readers with friends and family through her stories while inspiring her audience to serve others. Her tagline is *Inspiring Service Through Story*. As a member of American Christian Fiction Writers, she was named a Finalist in the 2017 First Impressions Contest and a Semi-Finalist in the 2018 and 2019 Genesis Contests.

Before writing, Laurie earned a bachelor's degree in both athletic training and exercise science and later obtained her master's degree in health promotion and education. She now writes full time and lives with her husband and their two daughters in Cincinnati. For a week or two each summer, they enjoy discovering new adventures along the western coast of Michigan. Connect with Laurie on her website, Facebook, Instagram, and Twitter.

Dear Reader,

Thank you for picking up *Pockets of Promise*. I hope you enjoyed reading Mariah's story as much as I enjoyed writing it.

Inspiration for the book originated from an image of a quilt I saw on Facebook. In the hopes of helping our daughters who were grieving the loss of two grandparents, I started writing the story about a seventh-grade girl. When I pitched the idea to my agent, she instead strongly suggested I consider telling the story from the point of view of a young Amish woman during her *Rumspringa*. I'm so glad I followed her advice!

Proverbs 19:20 says, "Listen to advice and accept discipline, and at the end you will be counted among the wise." While living our lives, we don't always make the best decisions. As Mariah's grandmother said, "A mistake here and there doesn't make you a bad person. How you react after making a mistake matters more than what you did." Thankfully, we can learn from our errors, as well as from those who have gone through similar experiences before us.

Like Mariah, Grandma Mast, and Aunt Birdie, we all face tough decisions regardless of our age—decisions that may ultimately affect the lives of those around us: what to do after graduation, which job offer to accept, who to marry, how to best raise our children and care for aging parents. God surrounds us with the people we need during those different seasons.

Who is the wise person from whom you seek counsel? Maybe you don't see someone filling that role during this season of your life, and you're feeling alone. I hope you find comfort in knowing that you are not alone, for God is always with you. May you feel His presence in the days to come.

I'd love to hear from you. Please visit my website www.lauri-estroupsmith.com or connect with me on social media. I'm currently writing *Pockets of Purpose*, Book #2 in *The Pocket Quilt Series*. In this story, Dixie Yoder, Luke's sister in Book #1, travels from Pinecraft to Holmes County in search of a lasting love. I can't wait to introduce you to her hero!

Blessings and many thanks to you,

Laurie

MEET GRANDMA STROUP BARKER

Nancy Alta Steele Stroup Barker, 1906-2008

In *Pockets of Promise*, Grandma Mast and Aunt Birdie blessed Mariah by sharing wisdom with her. One such person in my life was my paternal grandmother, who passed away six weeks shy of her 102nd birthday. She lived her days as a faithful child of God, and she also made the best peanut butter fudge! Even today, whether in a grocery store or an Amish bakery, the sight of that rich, golden brown candy reminds me of her.

In honor of her memory, I thought it'd be fun to include a scene in the book where Aunt Birdie asks Mariah to help her whip up a batch of fudge. I'm happy to share my grandma's recipe with you, and I've included the little notes she jotted on the index card to guide me through the process. Since the recipe calls for marshmallow creme, her version tastes similar to Amish peanut butter spread. I hope you enjoy!

Peanut Butter Fudge

Ingredients:

2 cups granulated white sugar
2/3 cup milk *On occasion, I use skim milk.*
1 cup marshmallow creme
1 cup peanut butter

Directions:

1. In a medium saucepan, combine the sugar and milk. While stirring, bring the mixture to a boil on low heat.
2. Test for soft ball stage about three to four minutes after the mixture comes to a rolling boil. *I don't have a candy thermometer, so I drop a few drops of the syrup (the sugar-milk mixture) into a cup of ice water. The droplets will form a soft ball on the end of your finger. If you do have a candy thermometer, the mixture reaches soft ball stage between 234ºF and 240ºF.*
3. Remove the saucepan from the heat and add marshmallow creme and peanut butter to the mixture.
4. Stir until it begins to thicken.
5. Pour into a well-greased pan. *I use a 9"x 9" pan, but you can use what you want.*
6. Nuts can be added, if desired.
7. Let cool and cut.

Store in an airtight container at room temperature.

WITH THANKS

To Shelley Shepard Gray: For reading that first story and recognizing my potential between the lines. If not for your nudge to pursue writing, this book wouldn't exist. I'm thankful for your friendship.

To Julie Gwinn, my agent: For taking a chance on me, for your continued encouragement through the rejections, and for believing this would happen.

To the team at Vinspire Publishing: Dawn Carrington, for giving me this opportunity and for helping me navigate new waters. Becca Shreves, for your editing expertise and your careful consideration of the story and its characters. Elaina Lee with For the Muse Designs, for designing this beautiful cover and giving me exactly what I said I'd be excited to see.

To the authors in the ACFW community as well as those who write Amish fiction, I will be forever grateful for the wisdom and encouragement you have shared with me. I'd specifically like to recognize Amy Clipston, Suzanne Woods Fisher, and Kathleen Fuller for the advice and support they offered along the way.

To Vannetta Chapman, Kelly Irvin, and Carrie Schmidt: A huge thanks to the three of you for taking time out of your busy schedules to read Mariah's story and offering an endorsement for the book. I am blessed by your words.

To the Monday Morning Writers Group: you were among the first to hear Mariah's story, and I truly appreciate the suggestions you offered to strengthen the characters and enhance the plot.

To Holly Wilson for reading the early drafts of Grandma's letters and offering ways to improve the messages. And to Christa Metz for ensuring the story sounded believable and authentic.

To Cyndi, Darlene, Lisa, and Megan: Who would have thought when we started meeting over ten years ago to discuss kids and books that I would one day hand you something I wrote and ask you for a critique?

To Laura Brandenburg and Serena Crompton, my critique partners: through your detailed comments in the margins, you have helped me grow as a writer and a storyteller. I am grateful to God for crossing our paths, and I treasure our friendships.

To Jay: thanks for climbing on the back of the jet ski with me when Travis wouldn't. I'm sorry I flung you across the lake.

To the Life Group: I thank God for intertwining our lives. Calley and Catie, for being the sisters I never had and for reading the manuscript before I sent it to the editor. Matt, for your creative eye and for sharing your no-nonsense approach to being successful in business endeavors. Randy, for your love and for always giving me a reason to laugh.

To my parents: Mom, for reading every page of those early drafts and offering your unconditional support. Dad, for ensuring I had a strong foundation of faith early in life.

To our girls: for keeping me on track when my characters are too perfect and for reading over my shoulder and offering your opinions. More often than not, I went with your suggestions.

To Travis: for supporting each and every one of my crazy endeavors and for modeling for our daughters and me what it looks like to be a hero.

To The Author of the Story: For calling me out of the darkness and giving me purpose. May You have all the glory.

GET INVOLVED
SAVE THE TURTLES

There are five species of sea turtles swimming in waters surrounding Florida: Green Turtle, Hawksbill Turtle, Kemp's ridley, Leatherback Turtle, and Loggerhead Turtle. All five species are listed as either endangered or threatened. Female sea turtles nest every two to three years, and they make between 40,000 and 84,000 nests. They dig a hole and deposit 80 to 120 eggs in each nest, but only about one in 1,000 turtles survives into adulthood.

Learn more about sea turtle conservation efforts in the Florida Keys, by visiting:
Florida Fish and Wildlife Conservation Commission:
https://myfwc.com/research/wildlife/sea-turtles/
Key West Aquarium:
https://www.keywestaquarium.com/florida-keys-sea-turtles
Mote Marine Laboratory and Aquarium:
https://mote.org/
Save-A-Turtle:
https://www.save-a-turtle.org/
Sea Turtle Conservancy:
https://conserveturtles.org/category/florida/
World Wildlife Fund:
https://www.worldwildlife.org/

HELP AN AUTHOR

If you enjoyed reading *Pockets of Promise*, I would appreciate it if you would help others enjoy this book, too. Here are some of the ways you can help spread the word:

Lend it. This book is lending enabled so please share it with a friend.

Recommend it. Help other readers find this book by recommending it to friends, readers' groups, book clubs, and discussion forums.

Share it. Let other readers know you've read the book by positing a note to your social media account and/or your Goodreads account.

Review it. Please tell others why you liked this book by reviewing it on your favorite ebook site.

Everything you do to help others learn about my book is greatly appreciated!

Laurie Stroup Smith

PLAN YOUR NEXT ESCAPE!

WHAT'S YOUR READING PLEASURE?

Whether it's captivating historical romance, intriguing mysteries, young adult romance, illustrated children's books, or uplifting love stories, Vinspire Publishing has the adventure for you!

For a complete listing of books available, visit our website at www.vinspirepublishing.com.

Like us on Facebook at
www.facebook.com/VinspirePublishing

Follow us on Twitter at
www.twitter.com/vinspire2004

and follow our blog for details of our upcoming releases, giveaways, author insights, and more! www.vinspirepublishingblog.com.

We are your travel guide to your next adventure!